Matchbox Dreams

Book 1: The Drapkin kids in Dreamland

DOUGLAS SCHWARTZ

FOREWORD

(For parents to read before reading the first story)
About Dreams
What Do Toddlers Dream About?
By Dr. Harvey Karp

From infants to adults, everyone dreams. Psychologist David Foulkes studies children (from tots to teens) to bring the secrets of their dreams to the light of day. In his lab, he lets kids fall asleep and then wakes them three times a night—sometimes in REM and sometimes in NREM—and asks them to describe what they recall.

Foulkes' findings are surprising...in how unsurprising they are. Basically, little kids have little dreams. But exactly what kids see while dreaming depends on their age. As children develop and grow, their dreams do too.

Toddler dreams are usually just snapshots, looking much more like a slide show than a movie when compared to the dreams of adults.

They heavily feature animals and other familiar sights, like images of people eating. According to Foulkes, "Children's dream life...seems to be similar to their waking imagination and narration," he explains in his study, *Children's Dreaming and the Development of Consciousness*. "Animals carry human concerns and readily become objects of identification."

Understandably, dreams can confuse small kids. Pre-schoolers often think their dreams are magically placed in their heads by someone else, or by God.

What Do Children Dream About? (Ages 5 to 9)

In this age range, kids begin seeing moving images and characters in action. Dreams now include multiple events strung together, one after the other. Kids start developing greater ability to remember dreams. Still, that's not always the case: When roused during REM sleep, 25% of the kids in Foulkes' studies had no recollection of dreaming, a trend that continues through age 9.

Are you wondering what your kids are doing in their dreams? Good question, but the answer is…nothing! The "character of the self" hasn't even made an appearance yet!

Drumroll please…. Generally around age 8, children appear as central characters in their dreams. Dream narratives become more complex and longer. Not only do children dream up the action as it unfolds, they also have thoughts and feelings within the dream. While dreaming continues to evolve somewhat through the teenage years, Foulkes concludes that 9-year-olds are relatively mature dreamers!

So, Who Has the Sweetest Dreams of All?

It turns out that, on the balance, children do have happier dreams than adults. Foulkes found grown-up dreams often contain aggression and misfortune. In contrast, children's dreams are embroidered with positive emotions. https://www.happiestbaby.com/

Reading with Your Child

By: Bernice Cullinan, Brod Bagert

Start Young and Stay with It

Children learn to love the sound of language before they even notice the existence of printed words on a page. Reading books aloud to children stimulates their imagination and expands their understanding of the world. It helps them develop language and listening skills and prepares them to understand the written word. When the rhythm and melody of language become a part of a child's life, learning to read will be as natural as learning to walk and talk.

Even after children learn to read by themselves, it's still important for you to read aloud together. By reading stories that are on their interest level, but beyond their reading level, you can stretch young readers' understanding and motivate them to improve their skills.

It's Part of Life

Although the life of a parent is often hectic, you should try to read with your child at least once a day at a regularly scheduled time. But don't be discouraged if you skip a day or don't always keep to your schedule. Just read to your child as often as you possibly can.

If you have more than one child, try to spend some time reading alone with each child, especially if they're more than 2 years apart. However, it's also fine to read to children at different stages and ages at the same time. Most children enjoy listening to many types of stories. When stories are complex, children can still get the idea and can be encouraged to ask questions. When stories are easy or familiar, youngsters enjoy these "old friends" and may even help in the reading.

Talking about Stories

It's often a good idea to talk about a story you are reading, but you need not feel compelled to talk about every story. Good stories will encourage a love for reading, with or without conversation. And sometimes children need time to think about stories they have read. A day or so later, don't be surprised if your child mentions something from a story you've read together.

Taking the time to read with your children on a regular basis sends an important message: Reading is worthwhile.
http://www.readingrockets.org/article/reading-your-child

Table of Contents

Introduction for Parents

About matchbox dreams:

Matchbox Dreams is a collection of short stories developed to be read by an adult or older sibling to a child between the ages of 3 and 10 years old before a nap or bedtime. The goal is to give the child a head-start on what to dream about by reading a short story that takes place in Dreamland. This book contains a series of 20 short stories with a new book available every few months.

These stories may also spark the interest of older children since they are written at a high enough level to engage the adult reader as well as the children being read to.

Many of the stories will simultaneously be informative and entertaining for both the children and the reader. Woven into the stories will be examples of positive behavior, positive character traits and other messages which will reinforce children to be respectful of others and to be honest. There are no witches, dangerous animals, monsters or other characters which may cause nightmares in young children.

The first series of stories are built around two incredibly adorable mice called Harper and Remy. Later in the book, Millie joins in.

Each night, Harper, Remy and Millie will come alive through the short stories while your child holds and play-acts with them. The stories are designed to be around 10-15 minutes. Some chapters may be longer so feel free to stop and continue the chapter on another evening.

Although you don't need to purchase the toy mice to enjoy the stories, the stuffed animals will help children imagine the journeys to Dreamland, and they may assist with the children going to sleep faster and without as much effort on your part.

Children today get more than enough screen time but not enough imagination time. As the stories are read, there are no photos or illustrations to look at; children must recreate the story in their mind, acting out the story with the aid of Harper and Remy if they wish.

One goal of *Matchbox Dreams* is to help kids go to bed smoothly, which is a task that many kids struggle with. Getting your child into a consistent nighttime routine is critical and has many benefits. There have been multiple studies done, looking at how sleep affects children. An article from Parents.com mentions a British study that looked at the sleeping patterns of children between the ages of 3 and 7. They found links between consistent bedtime and positive behavior. They also found that irregular bedtimes interrupt a child's circadian rhythm, which then affects the mental and physical function of a child.

While this information may seem obvious to some, parents are not paying as much attention to it as they need to. In today's world, many parents let their kid(s) watch TV or play on an iPad before bedtime. While this does keep them occupied, it throws off their sleep schedule because the brightness of the screen can delay the body from releasing melatonin, a sleep hormone.

With *Matchbox Dreams*, there are no screens or images, so all your child must do is rest in their bed, close their eyes and listen to the adventure that awaits. Hopefully, *Matchbox Dreams* can become a part of your child's bedtime routine and help to encourage them to fall asleep quickly so they can join their friends in Dreamland.

At the end of each story, you should factor in another five to ten minutes to either play-act with your child or allow him/her to play alone. At a specified time, the child should be instructed to tuck the mice into their little beds placed near your child's pillow so your child, and the mice, can all enter Dreamland together.

Harper, Remy and Millie are recommended for children three years and older. With children younger than three, you can allow the child to play with Harper and Remy while reading. After the story is over, you can use the mice to play-act with your child and when your child is ready for sleep, take the little critters with you, telling your child they are going off to Dreamland.

Resources:

https://www.parents.com/health/healthy-happy-kids/young-children-behave-better-when-they-have-a-consistent-bedtime/

https://www.sleepfoundation.org/articles/why-electronics-may-stimulate-you-bed

About the Author

Douglas Schwartz started creating stories about a character called Mr. Hamster when his two daughters were just toddlers. Each night, Mr. Hamster would find himself in a new adventure. These adventures, made up on the spot, would give his daughters something to feed their imaginations and dreams, helping them sleep nightmare-free.

One possible reason for having sweet dreams instead of nightmares is that the stories had a central figure: a cute and loveable animal. The bedtime stories would help them start to imagine an adventure that would frequently carry on into dream time. Now, with his daughters grown up, and each with three children, he has been enlisted again to start creating stories to be read to their children.

Douglas decided to build the first series of adventures around three cute vintage mice: Harper, Remy and Millie. Harper, Remy and Millie will become an important part of your child's memories and will hopefully survive to be handed down to their children, not only as collectible toys, but as little friends for life.

Douglas graduated with a degree in psychology and a master's degree in mass communication. He currently resides in Northern California and soon plans on traveling between the two coasts to visit his daughters and grandchildren. One family lives in Florida and the other is in California. During his travels, new books will be developed in twenty-story installments and available to be downloaded to your Kindle reader.

For this book, Evie, a toddler; Constance, an intelligent four-year-old; and Titus, an adventurous six-year-old, will be the leading children from the real world. They will be whisked back to 1900 when Harper, Remy and Millie were created.

Please feel free to change the names of the children, as well as any other events that may make the stories more personalized to your children or grandchildren.

About Harper, Remy and Millie

Harper   Remy   Millie

M eet Harper, Remy and later in the story Millie, the dearest of friends through mischief and mirth, and the most divine mice on Earth. Each toy comes with a small plush mouse stuffed animal wearing a removable outfit, as well as a matching miniature blanket and pillow that nestle neatly inside the vintage-themed matchbox. Designed to foster creativity through pretend play, the Matchbox Mice reflect Foothill Toy Co's philosophy that simple toys create the purest joy.

More than meets the eye, each Matchbox Mouse playset is an invitation to a world where anything is possible. The vintage-inspired dress-up stuffed animals encourage imagination and the sort of make-believe play many parents will remember from their childhoods.

Foothill Toy Company crafts timeless treasures that kindle the imagination. Inspired by the classic toys of times past, they are aimed to deliver the magic of childhood, one Matchbox Mouse at a time.

FIRST STORY

(OKAY, NOW YOU CAN READ OUT LOUD)

CHAPTER 1

The Introduction of Harper, Remy and Millie

Harper, Remy and Millie aren't your typical stuffed animals. They possess the ability to come alive in Dreamland. Oh yes, Dreamland is real. It exists in your mind, but it only comes alive when you are sleeping. Just like how the night is never around during the day, Dreamland is only around when you are sleeping.

So, what about daydreaming, you may ask, or what about pretend play? Well, Harper, Remy and Millie love to be with you when you are daydreaming or pretending, but they will just look and act like all your other stuffed animals and toys.

The real magic begins when you go to bed. As soon as you fall asleep, Harper, Remy and Millie, tucked into their little beds and snuggled up safe and warm by your side, wake up and begin a new adventure each night. Some experiences are so much fun, you may want to relive them again and again.

Like all adventures, there needs to be a beginning. For Harper and Remy and later Millie, the beginning started a very long time ago.

It was before you were born, before your mom and dad were born and even before your grandparents were born.

Harper and Remy got their start in 1900, at the turn of a new century, in a small village at the foothills of Boise, Idaho. A young toymaker named Jack wanted to create cute toys for his three children: his youngest Evie, his middle child Constance and his oldest Titus.

With snow all around his little cabin, his wife at the sewing machine and the children tucked in bed, Jack worked at his small workbench near the only fireplace in the cabin. Jack was sketching animals, which he and his wife could make as toys and sell at the store he worked at. You see, Jack started each day working at the local toy store, stocking shelves and selling toys to children in the village.

Each night, he would remember the expressions on the children's faces when they received their new toys. He used this knowledge to design what he thought would be the most desired toys in the world.

Jack noticed that small stuffed animals like mice, hamsters and puppies were the most popular toys with the children in the village. With that information, that night, he was inspired to create a couple of the cutest stuffed toys anyone had ever owned.

As it got later, Jack's wife, Mrs. Drapkin, kissed Jack on the cheek and said she was going to sleep. Soon after, Jack started yawning from all his hard work. It didn't help that he was also really cozy in his chair near the fireplace. He soon put his head down on the workbench and fell fast asleep.

In the olden times, people didn't dream unless the Sandman visited them. And for the Sandman to come to your house, everyone had to be sleeping. Unlike Santa Claus, the Sandman could not get to every home in one night, so some nights, people just didn't dream.

With everyone in the Drapkin house fast asleep and the Sandman being in Idaho, he stopped by to sprinkle dream dust on each member of the family. When he got to Jack, he looked at the cute mice Jack had drawn on his sketch pad, and he accidentally spilled dream dust on the drawings. Later that night, Jack had a most colorful dream, like the kind he used to have as a kid. He dreamt he was in Dreamland, and he was being shown around by the two mice he had drawn in his sketchpad.

Harper, one of the mice, came up to Jack and said, "Hi, I am Harper, and this is my sister Remy."

"Wow, you can speak," said Jack. "You look exactly like the mice I was drawing."

"Well, when you were young, you probably went to our part of Dreamland, and you must have seen us there and remembered us," Remy replied. "Since the Sandman spilled dream dust on our sketch, now whenever anyone sleeps near us, they can join us in Dreamland even if the Sandman didn't visit their home."

Harper added, "Our part of Dreamland is usually just for kids, but since you design toys for kids, you can enter Dreamland even though you are a grown-up."

"Yes," Jack said, "now I remember. When I was young, I did visit Dreamland. I guess now when I dream, I go somewhere else."

"You are correct," said Remy. "Dreamland is just one part of Dreamworld, which has many different lands. When you sleep, you go to one of those other lands. They can be fun, but Dreamland is the nicest, safest and most fun land in of all Dreamworld." Remy continued, "There are no monsters, witches or ghosts in Dreamland, and there are lots of places to travel, adventures to be had and people and animals to meet."

"How long have you two been living in Dreamland?" asked Jack.

"Well, we are not sure," said Harper. "Ever since we can remember, we have been here. Time is different in Dreamland. Instead of having the past, present and future, we can visit all three times anytime we want."

Remy added, "We would show you around, but it may be best for you to wake up now while we are fresh in your memory, so you can finish the sketches and make us into real stuffed animals."

"Yes," said Harper, "and when you make us, please make us nice beds that we can sleep in while we travel off to Dreamland."

Jack woke up. He sat up in his chair and thought to himself that his dream was one of the most real dreams he had ever had. He had forgotten what a beautiful place Dreamland was. Then he looked down at his sketches and noticed a small pile of sparkling dust on each drawing. He paused. Had it all been a dream, or did it really happen?

That night, Jack finished his sketches of Harper and Remy, and in the morning, he gave the drawings to Mrs. Drapkin so she could make the two mice with her sewing machine. While Mrs. Drapkin was lighting the fire to make breakfast, she ran out of matches and was about to throw the empty matchbox in the fireplace when Jack told her to save it. He thought it was a perfect size for Harper and Remy's bed, so he asked Mrs. Drapkin for another one.

All during the day while Jack was working at the toy store, he kept thinking about the dream he had the night before and about how real it had seemed. When he got home, he couldn't wait to see what Mrs. Drapkin had sewn up while he was at work.

Sitting on his workbench were two large matchboxes. On the outside of each box, Mrs. Drapkin had drawn three mice pedaling a three mouse-powered bicycle under the name Royal Star Brand. He slowly opened the first box to see Harper tucked snuggly between his bed and blanket smiling up at him. He opened the second box and found Remy tucked into bed, smiling too.

Although Jack had left his wife detailed sketches of Harper and Remy, he was surprised at how every detail was exactly like the Harper and Remy of his dream. At dinner time, when his wife and three children—Evie, Constance and Titus—were eating, he showed them Harper and Remy and told everyone about the dream he had the night before. The kids instantly fell in love with the mice and asked their dad if they could have them.

Jack had planned on taking Harper and Remy to the toy store the next day to see if Mr. Lambert, the owner of the store, wanted to place an order of copies of Harpers and Remys to sell in the store.

"Titus, since you are the oldest, you can pick which mouse you want to sleep with tonight," Jack said. Titus picked Harper. Constance was happy because secretly she wanted Remy anyway. Evie was too young to speak, but Jack could tell she was not happy being left out of choosing a mouse.

"Evie, you are too young to be able to sleep with Harper or Remy, but when I read to all of you tonight, you can each take turns playing with the mice," said Jack. "Evie, in a few days when you turn three years old, you can have your own mouse." Evie seemed happy with that decision.

For the first time in ages, all three of the children had all their chores done, their teeth brushed, their faces washed and they were in bed even before Mrs. Drapkin had to ask them.

It was the Drapkin family tradition to gather all the children together in one bed and for Jack to tell a story each evening. Most of the time, he would make up stories based around the stuffed animals in the toy store. This evening, Jack told them about his trip to Dreamland and how he met Harper and Remy. He also told them what Remy had said: if the mice were tucked into their little matchboxes and sleeping near you at night, you could enter Dreamland anytime, even if the Sandman had not sprinkled dream dust on you.

Constance and Titus could not wait to fall asleep so they could start dreaming. Right after Jack told them a story, both children said they were tired and ready for bed. Constance took Remy to her bedroom and Titus took Harper to his. Poor Evie didn't have a new mouse to sleep with, so when Jack tucked her into her crib, she snuggled up to her old stuffed hamster doll that Jack called Mr. Hamster.

After everyone was tucked into bed, Jack went and sat by the fireplace with Mrs. Drapkin. Meanwhile, Titus took Harper out of his matchbox and told Harper that when he slept that night, he would like to go to Dreamland like his dad did and have Harper show him around. Harper continued to smile up at Titus in response. Before Titus fell asleep, he pretended that Harper was walking through sand dunes (his blankets) and that Harper could fly wherever he wanted to.

In the other room, Constance was doing the same thing, only she pretended that her blankets were knee-high soft green grass that she and Remy were making their way through to find Titus and Harper. After a while, both Constance and Titus grew tired, so they tucked their new little friends into their matchbox beds, and both fell fast asleep.

CHAPTER 2

Dreamland

Within minutes of falling asleep, Titus was standing on the beach looking out over the ocean. He was so excited to be at the ocean since it was almost 400 miles from his cottage.

"Isn't the sea pretty?" said Constance.

Titus looked to his right and saw Constance and Evie standing on the beach near him, holding hands and watching the seagulls swooping down over the waves looking for small fish to eat.

"Constance, how did we get to the ocean?" asked Titus. "The last thing I remember was putting Harper to sleep in his bed near my pillow."

"Yep," said Harper. "That's what you did right before falling asleep. Now you are in Dreamland."

Titus turned around to see Harper and Remy standing right behind them. "Harper how did you get so big?" asked Titus. "You are almost the same size as me!"

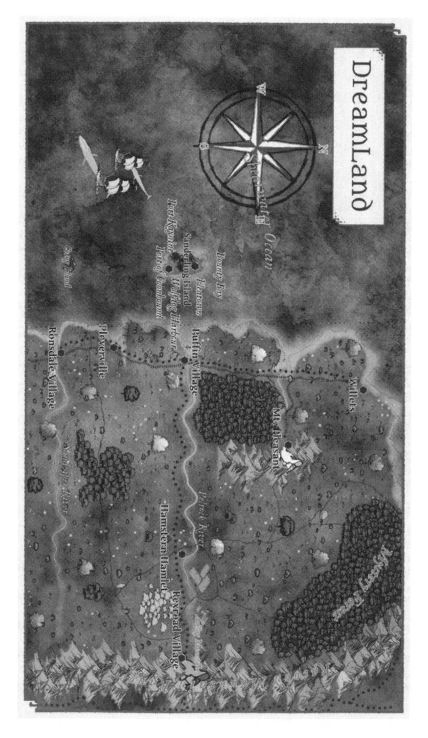

"Well, actually, we didn't get big. You, Constance and Evie got small," said Harper. "Whenever you visit Dreamland, you are the same size as your animal friends."

Constance said, "Hey Titus, Harper is right. Either that or these seashells are gigantic." She let out a giggle and pointed to seashells that were ten times their usual size.

"So, what part of Dreamland are we in?" Titus asked.

"Harper and I live in Puffin Village, which is just over the other side of the dunes behind us, heading east," declared Remy. "To the north, up the coast, is the town of Willetts where the squirrel clan lives. To the south is Ploverville, where the kittens live, and the ocean to the west is called Shearwater. About 50 miles out to sea is the beautiful island of Sanderling, home of the puppies."

"Hey everyone," Harper said, "do you want to come to our house for tea and cookies?"

"Sure," said Evie. Titus and Constance stared at Evie in confusion.

Both said at the same time, "Evie, you can't speak yet; you're too young."

"Remember, this is Dreamland where everything is possible," declared Harper.

With that, everyone started to walk up the dunes towards Harper and Remy's house in Puffin Village. Their home was more of a burrow in the ground than a real house. Imagine a whole village with a village center, a large fountain and shops constructed of boards made from driftwood with water-worn glass for windows. Radiating out in all directions from the village center, like a wagon wheel, were white lanes paved with small particles of broken shells and large grains of sand. These lanes went from the village center to the hills that surrounded Puffin Village. In the hills were hundreds of little burrows. Each burrow was decorated with colorful shells, glass, driftwood fences and other items that had been found on the beach. One burrow, exceptionally large and ornate, caught Constance's attention.

"Remy, whose house is that?" inquired Constance.

"That house belongs to Mr. Downing, the mayor of Puffin Village," said Remy. "The mayor is going up to Willets this week to meet with the mayor of the squirrels. Last week, some of the squirrels came to Puffin looking to purchase nuts, and one of the younger squirrels accidentally knocked over Mr. Springer's nut cart, causing all his roasted nuts to fall in the street. Before Mr. Springer could catch the youngster, he and his friends took off up a tree and jumped from tree to tree until they were out of Puffin Village. Mr. Downing is going to be traveling there soon to meet with the mayor of Willets to collect payment for the soiled nuts."

After a ten-minute walk, they arrived at Harper and Remy's home. Since the kids were the same size as the mice, they had no trouble entering the house and sitting down at the dinner table. Harper started the fire in the fireplace while Remy lit the stove.

21

Being that it was still 1900 in Dreamland, homes had yet to have electricity. Electricity, invented in 1882, didn't make it to Dreamland until the late 1920s when kids in the real world started getting electricity to their homes and began dreaming about things like electric lights, electric stoves, and electric heaters.

Soon, the water was boiling, and Remy served everyone tea while Harper took the cookie jar down from the cupboard and gave each person a peanut butter cookie.

"These cookies are great," said Titus. "Can I have another, please?"

"I like this tea. What is it called?" asked Constance.

"You can have as many cookies as you want, Titus," said Remy. "After all, it is your dream. Constance, this is dandelion tea. We use the whole dandelion, petals, stem, roots and all to make the tea. One dandelion will last us over a month, even if we drink it every day."

After everyone had all the cookies and tea they could eat and drink, they got up to look around the house. Titus had six cookies, Constance had three and little Evie surprised everyone by eating 8 cookies. Now that Evie could speak, her favorite words were "more please."

First, they descended a rickety staircase made of wood planks and driftwood to the root cellar. Since they did not have electricity, Remy brought a candle with her made from beeswax and an old yo-yo string. The cellar was large and damp and in between the roots were shelves lined with all kinds of yummy-looking jars of food. There were jars of cherries floating in a reddish liquid, peanut butter, grape jelly, and cans of peas, corn, and string beans, and there were burlap bags of every type of nut you could think of.

From the root cellar, they ascended to the ground floor where the kitchen, library and living room were. They continued up another flight of stairs to the bedrooms and bathroom. From the bedroom window, they could see an old sailing ship parked in the backyard.

"Harper, why do you have a ship in the backyard?" asked Titus.

"A few years ago, there was a large storm and a wave brought the ship all the way over the dunes to our backyard," said Harper. "Do you want to go aboard?"

Without a word, but with shouts of glee, all three of the kids rushed down the stairs and were climbing the ladder to get aboard the ship.

The ship had three masts with the sails wrapped up, a large deck and the captain's quarters in the back.

"This is great!" said Titus. "All the charts and furnishings are still here. What happened to the captain and crew?"

"We don't know," said Remy. "The ship washed up here like you see it, and we were never able to locate the owner."

"Do you think we can sail it to Sanderling Island someday to see the puppies?" asked Constance.

"Sure, all you have to do is dream about it when you are here some night, and the ship will be ready to go," responded Remy.

Titus, Constance and Evie spent the rest of the time exploring the ship. Below the deck, there were twenty cannons, thirty hammocks for the crew to sleep in, a galley to cook food and a large area under the deck stocked with all kinds of food and provisions for a long trip.

Titus climbed all the way to the top of the tallest mast and made his way into the crow's nest. From there, he could see all of Puffin Village and how the village did, in fact, look like a wagon wheel.

"Harper, do you think this used to be a pirate ship?" asked Titus.

"It could have been," answered Harper. "We did find some treasure aboard, which is now hidden in one of the caves up in those hills."

"Can we go looking for the hidden treasure today?" Titus asked excitedly.

"We should probably make that a different dream," responded Harper with a soft chuckle. "It is a long walk, and we will need to have supplies to take with us."

Just as Titus was checking out the deck, he heard an alarm go off. Titus turned to Harper and asked him why an alarm was going off.

"That is your alarm at home telling you to wake up, so you can get ready for school," said Harper.

"But I don't want to leave," protested Titus with a pout. "I like it here in Dreamland, and there is so much to see! What about Constance and Evie? Do they have to wake up too?"

"No," said Remy. "They don't have school yet, so they can stay longer."

Just as Titus was about to protest again, he woke up, looked around and realized he was in his bedroom. He hit the top of his alarm harder than usual to turn it off and got out of bed. He almost went to wake up Constance and Evie too, so they would have to leave Dreamland, but he decided that was not a nice thing to do, so he went off the kitchen to see what his mom had prepared for him for his breakfast, still thinking about the magical land he had just come from.

CHAPTER 3

The Birthday Party

That night, Titus could not wait to return to Dreamland. After dinner, and after taking baths, Titus, Constance and Evie all gathered in one bed so Jack could tell them another story. After the story, Constance took Remy to her bedroom, and Titus took Harper to his bedroom. Jack and Mrs. Drapkin went into each child's room, said prayers, gave them big hugs, got each child water and tucked them in bed. Constance and Titus made sure to tuck their new friends into their little beds and lay down to go to sleep. They were so excited about revisiting Dreamland that they fell asleep fast. They didn't even play with their friends; they just laid their heads down on their pillows and were soon fast asleep.

"Hey Remy, it looks like Titus, Constance and Evie, our friends from the real world, may be coming to Mayor Downing's birthday party today," said Harper.

"Yay! It is always great to have new friends to go on adventures and to share birthday cake with," said Remy with a big smile.

Puffin Village is big on birthday parties. You see., no matter whose birthday it is, weather permitting (which is almost always permitting in Dreamland, unless of course you like cold and rain and want to dream about that), the whole village gets together in the village center and has a party. For each birthday, Mrs. Wilson, owner and chief baker at Mrs. Wilson's Bakery, makes a large cake for everyone in the village to share.

Titus, Constance and Evie woke up in the middle of Puffin Village surrounded by hundreds of villagers. The sun was shining, and there were hundreds of mice dressed in colorful outfits, all standing around and waiting for something to happen.

Constance turned to a mouse, wearing a beautiful floral dress with a yellow straw hat, and whispered, "What are we all waiting for?"

"Oh, how rude of me. I didn't introduce myself. My name is Kim, and I am Harper and Remy's next-door neighbor. Today is the mayor's birthday, and Harper and Remy are just up there by the giant birthday cake waiting for the mayor to officially start the party. Once the mayor gives his speech, he will cut the cake, and Harper and Remy will come over here and show you around Puffin Village," Kim went on to say.

"Ladies and gentlemice," Mayor Downing exclaimed with his outside voice, "today we are gathered here to celebrate my birthday. It seems like only yesterday I came to live here in Puffin Village. Since then, we have had hundreds of children from the real world visit and teach us things we would have never learned. I am very grateful for the knowledge they have taught us."

Mayor Downing went on to explain, "Many people, especially grown-ups, don't realize how much they can learn from children. Unlike teenagers, who think they already know everything, children learn new things every day, and they like to share what they learn with grown-ups. If grown-ups took the time to listen and speak with children, they would learn something new too. It may be something new the grown-ups didn't know, or it may be something they did know but forgot, as their minds get full of stuff as they get older. Grown-ups sometimes have so much in their minds, they take the old stuff and put it in the storage section of their minds to make room for more stuff. Sometimes, it takes a child to help a grown-up remember where a memory was stored."

Like many important people in towns and villages, Mayor Downing could talk for hours. So, before the mayor could continue with his speech, Mr. Springer, the town roasted nut vendor, started singing happy birthday to the mayor. Soon, everyone was singing, including Titus, Constance and Evie. They were singing so loudly, they drowned out Mayor Downing's speech, and even Mayor Downing joined in with the song. As everyone was singing, Mrs. Wilson cut the cake and passed out generous slices to everyone in the village. While she was passing the cake around, Harper and Remy made their way through the crowd over to Titus, Constance and Evie.

"Hello Harper and Remy," said Evie.

"Thanks for coming to the birthday party," Remy said. "Would all of you like to meet the mayor?"

"Sure, that would be great," said Constance.

"Can we eat our cake first? Do you have any ice cream? Also, can we have seconds?" Titus blurted out.

"Titus, you haven't even eaten the first slice yet," said Constance rolling her eyes.

After everyone had their two servings of cake with chocolate chip ice cream, they walked over to where the mayor was standing and eating his cake, and Harper introduced them to Mayor Downing. Mayor Downing was a robust mouse, shorter than Harper but way more rounded at the waist.

The mayor wore a black coat with tails and a gray vest with a silver watch chain attached to a button; the watch rested in his right-side vest pocket. Titus noticed that the mayor's tail poked out between the coattails. Titus started to giggle because every time the mayor talked, his tail would move around and sometimes get tangled up with the coattails. The mayor also had the longest set of whiskers Titus had ever seen. Titus figured the mayor put wax on his whiskers because they curled up on both sides and were almost as high as the mayor's ears.

"Harper, who do we have here?" asked Major Downing.

"These are my human friends from the real world," Harper explained. "This young lady is Constance; this young gentleman is Titus, and our little friend with cake all over her face and a dab of ice cream on the end of her nose is Evie."

Constance did her best curtsey, Titus bowed deeply, and Evie licked her lips and wiped her nose on her sleeve.

Before the mayor could say another word, Evie whispered to Constance that she had to go to the bathroom, so she was going to wake up and cry for her mom. Within seconds, Evie disappeared from Dreamland. Apparently, her crying also woke up Constance, because she disappeared too.

The mayor looked at Titus and said, "Do you need to return to the real world too?"

"Nah," Titus said. "Today is Saturday, so I am in no rush to wake up."

The mayor turned to Harper and said, "Harper, since you and I are traveling to Willets to collect money from Mayor Bushytail, of the squirrel clan, do you think your little friend wants to join us?"

Harper asked Titus, and Titus said that he was always up for an adventure.

"Harper, you should introduce Titus to some of your friends who are at my birthday party while I get ready to travel to Willets," Mayor Downing announced. "I will meet you and Titus at the train station in one hour. I have a reserved sleeper car, which will be big enough for all of us, so don't worry about booking reservations."

"Sounds good," said Harper. "See you in an hour." Harper brought Titus back to the stage in the village center where birthday cake crumbs and icing were spread all over the table and on the floor.

"Looks like all of the cake is gone. Any more ice cream left?" asked Titus curiously.

"No, it looks like that is gone too, but there will be lots to eat on the train," said Harper. Just as he said that, Mr. Springer, the roasted nut vendor, walked up to Harper and Titus.

"You must be Titus," asked Mr. Springer. "I knew your father. He was a great kid. I haven't seen him in years since he grew up and stopped coming to Dreamland."

"Father never mentioned that he came to Puffin Village when he was young," said Titus.

"Oh yes, this was before Harper and Remy joined us," said Mr. Springer. "Your father was quite a little adventurer," Mr. Springer added with a smirk.

"Do you remember any stories about him?" asked Titus.

"Well, there was one time that your dad was here with a friend he called Squirrely, a squirrel from Willets, and they were getting supplies from Mr. Nordmo's General Store to go on a trip to Ploverville to check out Kitten Village," said Mr. Springer.

"Anyhow, after they got their supplies, they loaded them in a new Ford horseless carriage that your dad had dreamt up for the trip. Everyone in the village was here to see them off since it was the first horseless carriage anyone had ever seen. Now, they are just referred to as cars.

"After the car was loaded up, Squirrely was in front turning the crank to start the car, and your dad was in the car pushing on the gas pedal. Well, the car started so fast that the crank began spinning and Squirrely was tossed high into the air. When he returned to earth, he landed in the water fountain way over there. Your dad was laughing so hard, he woke up, and he and the car disappeared from Dreamland," added Mr. Springer.

Just as Titus was going to ask about what more adventures his dad had gone on, Constance came into his room and woke him up for breakfast.

CHAPTER 4

Puffin Village

After breakfast, Titus and Constance went outside to do their chores in the barn. The weather was very cold, and there was snow piled high on the ground, but the sun was shining, and it looked like it was going to be a beautiful day. Titus took two pails for milking the cow, and Constance had a basket for collecting eggs. Little Evie was all bundled up with her hand-me-down coat from Constance, along with her pink gloves and matching hat her mother had knitted for her.

While Constance and Evie were collecting eggs, one of the eggs rolled under a loose plank on the floor. Constance asked Titus to get the egg, and when he lifted the plank, he found an old shoebox with a string around it. Titus pulled the string and opened the box. Inside, he found a small old tattered brown squirrel stuffed animal with a blue vest and a bushy tail.

Titus and Constance looked at each other and both came to the same conclusion that this must be Dad's stuffed animal for Dreamland. For the rest of the day, Titus and Constance couldn't wait for their dad to get home from work so they could ask him about the stuffed squirrel and his adventures in Dreamland.

After doing all the chores in the barn, cleaning their rooms and doing home-school studies with their mom, it was finally getting time for their dad to come home. Titus and Constance helped their mother set the table for dinner while Evie was in her high-chair nibbling on cut carrots. Mrs. Drapkin cooked a roast along with peeled potatoes from their garden, cooked carrots and homemade bread. Between the smell of the fireplace, cooked roast and homemade bread, everyone could hardly wait until dinner.

Finally, the front door opened, and Jack came in quickly to keep the snow and wind out of the house. "Dear, everything smells great! You must have been cooking all day," Jack said to his wife, giving her a kiss on the head.

"It wasn't that bad. Titus and Constance helped with cleaning and peeling the potatoes and carrots while I prepared the roast and made the bread," said Mrs. Drapkin.

"You kids are turning out to be great little helpers," said Jack, tousling Constance's hair.

Once they had sat down for dinner and said prayers, Titus and Constance both started asking their dad questions at the same time.

"Dad, I was in the barn searching for an egg when I found this stuffed squirrel stuffed animal," Titus declared, pulling the animal from his pocket.

"Was this your stuffed animal, and does it have anything to do with Dreamland?" inquired Constance.

"Titus, it is kind of late in the year for an Easter egg hunt," chuckled Jack.

"No, I wasn't hunting for eggs, Dad. I was retrieving an egg that Constance let roll under the floorboards in the barn," Titus said matter-of-factly.

Jack picked up the squirrel stuffed animal, brushed off some of the dust and straw and said, "Well, well, I haven't seen Squirrely since I was a kid. When I started going to high school, I put Squirrely in a shoebox for safekeeping, and I guess I completely forgot about him."

Titus and Constance looked at each other, then at their dad, and at the same time, they both asked, "Was Squirrely the Mayor of Willets when you were our age?"

"No," said Jack. "He was just a student like me back then. Wait!" Jack exclaimed. "How do you know about Willets?"

Titus and Constance both laughed and said that last night, they went to Puffin Village in Dreamland and learned about Willets and how the mayor of Puffin Village, Harper and Remy were going to go to Willets to meet Mayor Bushytail. They were going to collect money for Mr. Springer's roasted nut cart, which had been knocked over by a young squirrel.

"Squirrely's real name was Jim Bushytail. Everyone just called him Squirrely because he was always getting into trouble. I wonder if he is now the mayor of Willets," Jack added.

During this discussion, Mrs. Drapkin looked at Jack and the kids and said, "I think I missed something here. What are you all talking about? When I was young, I never went to that part of Dreamland."

"Dreamland is very large," said Jack. "Chances are, when you were young, you went to a different part of Dreamland. Did you have a stuffed animal you slept with when you were young?" Jack asked his wife.

"No," said Mrs. Drapkin. "When I was young, I slept with my favorite blanket."

"Well, that explains it," Jack went on to say. "You need a stuffed animal host to get into the part of Dreamland I used to go to." Titus and Constance nodded in agreement; at least that was their understanding on how to get to the fun part of Dreamland.

"That is true," Constance said. "Remy told me that If you go to Dreamland by yourself, you can end up anywhere. When you travel with a partner like Remy or Harper, or even Mayor Bushytail, you get to go to the best places in Dreamland where everything is fun and safe, and there are always new adventures to experience."

36

That evening, after the kids had cleaned off the table and gotten into bed, Jack thought he would tell them a funny story that happened to him when he was in Dreamland.

"Seeing Mr. Bushytail reminded me of an adventure I had when I was your age, Titus," started Jack. "One night, when I got to Willets, Squirrely and I had just finished riding the rapids in an old canoe we found. We pushed the canoe onto a small beach and got out to explore the area. No sooner had we climbed up the bank did we notice the canoe had broken loose and was floating downstream."

"What did you do?" asked a fascinated Constance.

"Well," said Jack, "seeing a long vine hanging from a nearby tree, I jumped on the vine, swung out over the water and yelled a Tarzan scream as loud as I could. But I soon learned that I didn't grab onto a vine at all but instead the nose of a very tall garaffant."

"What is a garaffant?" asked Titus, his eyebrows furrowed together.

"Imagine a giraffe, but instead of a long neck, it has a long nose like an elephant. It is the same color as an elephant too. Anyhow, when I grabbed the garaffant's nose I made him sneeze and he shot me into the river, past the canoe. It was like being shot out of a cannon, it was so fast.

"I was able to get into the canoe and, using the paddle, I made my way back to shore. Squirrely ran down to meet me to see if I was okay, but before he could ask me anything, he fell on the sand laughing so hard he almost couldn't catch his breath! At that point, I was getting a bit mad since I had just risked my life by being launched into the air by a strange-looking animal, so I didn't see what was so funny. Squirrely managed to stop laughing long enough to walk me over to a still pond near the river so I could see my reflection in the water. Besides being soaking wet, I had a large glob of purple stuff covering my hair, which later turned out to be garaffant slime, and there was a live fish stuck in the slime looking back at me in the reflection. Upon seeing this, I started to laugh so hard that I woke myself up, causing me to leave Dreamland," Jack told them while chuckling at the memory.

"Okay, now it's time for bed," Jack said.

"Wait," said Titus. "You can't stop there; what else happened?"

"I will try and remember more stories," Jack said, "but now it is time for everyone to go to sleep and make your own dreams."

Jack picked up Evie to carry her to her crib, and Mrs. Drapkin walked Titus and Constance to their rooms and tucked them into their beds. Titus tucked Harper into his matchbox bed, Constance tucked Remy into her bed, and they all went to sleep as fast as they could.

CHAPTER 5

Mr. Nordmo's General Store

Within minutes, Titus was back in Puffin Village. He looked around and didn't see Constance or Evie, so he assumed they had not fallen asleep yet.

A voice from behind Titus said, "I understand you are going to Willets with Harper and Mayor Downing to collect the money the squirrel clan owes me for knocking over my roasted nut cart." It was Mr. Springer. "Is this your first trip to Willets?" Mr. Springer went on to ask.

Titus said, "Yes, it will be."

Mr. Springer said, "Here is a large bag of roasted nuts for your trip. Please stop by when you get back, and I will give you another bag for your troubles."

Titus took the bag and went to put it in his pocket when he remembered his pajamas didn't have pockets. Harper noticed for the first time that Titus was wearing his flannel pajamas. He told Titus that the train they were going to ride to Willets was pretty fancy, so they should go over to Mr. Nordmo's General Store to pick out clothes for the trip.

Mr. Nordmo's General Store was less than a block from the village center. As they walked there, they passed Mrs. Wilson's Bakery, the Tuney Candy Store and the Cheese Barrel, which had cheeses from all over Dreamland.

"Harper, am I dreaming, or is the largest cheese store in the world?" Titus asked.

"Titus, everything in Dreamland is in your dreams, but this is the largest cheese store on the west coast of Dreamland," Harper said. "By the way, next time you come to Dreamland, instead of wearing your pajamas, you can dream up other clothes to wear so we don't have to go to Mr. Nordmo's General Store every time to get new clothes."

Stepping into Mr. Nordmo's General Store was like stepping back in time. The floor was made of old and uneven wooden planks that creaked every time Titus took a step. The counter was made of one large plank of walnut with a large scale to weigh things and an old-time cash register sitting on top. There were all kinds of farm tools hanging on the walls. On the floor, there were lots of barrels filled to the top with stuff. One had nails, another had flour, a third had apples, but the ones that Titus liked were the barrels filled with taffy candy.

"There must be fifty barrels of candy in all different colors," Titus said in amazement.

"Mr. Nordmo makes his own saltwater taffy candy, using ingredients from around Puffin Village," said Harper. "I think it is the best in Dreamland," he added.

Mr. Nordmo walked over to Titus and Harper and asked how he could be of assistance. Harper pointed to Titus' PJs and asked if Mr. Nordmo had anything more appropriate for a train trip. Mr. Nordmo brought Titus over to the clothing section, and Titus instantly spotted a cowboy outfit he really liked. While Titus was trying on the clothes, Harper was buying some supplies for the trip, including lots of candy and fruit to take along for snacks. Titus came over to the counter, dressed in blue jeans, a red and white plaid shirt, a tan vest, leather belt, leather boots and a large cowboy hat.

"Well, not entirely what I would have selected for this trip, but it fits you well," stated Harper. Harper told Mr. Nordmo to add it to his bill. After Harper paid for the clothes and supplies, they made their way to the train station.

Titus had the nuts Mr. Springer had given him in one vest pocket and the watermelon taffy candy Mr. Nordmo had given him for the trip in the other vest pocket. Titus was happy. He had a new cowboy outfit and lots of snacks, and he and his new friend Harper were going on an adventure.

The train station was a large, ornate brick building. Inside, it had a huge waiting area with beautiful mosaic tiles on the floor and murals that covered most of the walls. The murals showed different lands within Dreamland. While they were waiting for Mayor Downing, Harper was pointing to each of the lands and telling Titus about where each land was and which animals lived in each land.

Titus was looking at the map, which showed the train trip they were going on to Willets, and said to Harper, "Willets looks like quite a distance away. How long is it going to take get there?"

"It will probably take one night, so hopefully, when you go to sleep tomorrow evening, your dream will pick up where it left off, and you will be back on the train," Harper said.

"If this is a dream, how come we can't just click our heels together like Dorothy did in the *Wizard of OZ* and just arrive there instantly?" Titus asked.

Just as Titus finished saying that, Mayor Downing showed up and heard what Titus said. "That's the problem with all you real-worlders; you're always in a rush. Each night, you have hours and hours to dream, and all you want to do is go to new places. Well, most times, the journey leads to more adventures than the destination," said Mayor Downing.

Harper joined in and said, "What the mayor is saying is that the traveling part of the dream, or in the real world for that matter, can be as much or more fun than the actual place you are traveling to.

Wait until you see the inside of the train. I'm sure after you see it, you won't be in any rush to get to Willets."

The train conductor took Mayor Downing's luggage and showed them the way to the sleeper car. The train was like the one Titus had seen in old western movies. The floor was covered with thick red wool carpet with gold and blue patterns running the length of the car. The walls were a dark mahogany wood, polished to the point that Titus could see his reflection in it.

When they finally got to the sleeper car, Titus could not believe how much room there was. There were two large couches with a table in the middle and two beds up above the couches. The walls were the same mahogany wood and all the metal was made of brass.

"Harper, you're right. This is going to be a great trip. Can I please sit by the window?" asked Titus.

"Sure," said Harper. "Right after we pull out of the train station, I will show you the rest of the train."

Within minutes, the mayor was unpacked, Harper had placed some of the snacks on the table and the train started to roll out of the station. As the train began moving faster, Titus noticed it began rocking back and forth. At first, the rocking was light, then it got stronger and stronger to the point that Titus was being bounced around the sleeper car. Finally, Titus woke up to find that the rocking was Titus's mother trying to wake him.

"Titus, it's time to get up," his mother said. "You have been sleeping for over eight hours, and you need to have breakfast."

Needless to say, Titus was not happy to be woken up from his dream just when his adventure was about to begin.

"Mom, why did you wake me? I was just about to take a train trip to Willets with Harper and the mayor when you woke me up."

Titus's mother gave him an odd look and asked if he had a fever. She felt his forehead, and when she didn't feel one, she told Titus to get dressed.

During breakfast, Titus told Constance and Evie about what they missed in Dreamland. He told them about Mr. Nordmo's General Store, his new cowboy outfit, the saltwater watermelon taffy, about the large train station and the beautiful sleeper car. He thought Mayor Downing wouldn't mind if they all stayed in the sleeper car for the journey to Willets if Constance and Evie wanted to join him tonight in their dreams.

Constance and Evie really wanted to go on the trip to Willets with Titus, so the two bigger kids did all their chores, and while Constance cleaned her room, Titus took his bath and brushed his teeth. Constance then took her bath, brushed her teeth too and joined her siblings who were all sitting on the couch ready for Jack to read a new story about the adventures in Dreamland. They got ready for bed so fast that their parents hadn't even finished cleaning up the dinner dishes.

No sooner was the story over, and all three of the kids hugged their parents and said they were ready for bed. Mrs. Drapkin thought they may be suffering from a fever since it was rare for the kids to go to bed without a struggle. After feeling all their foreheads and not detecting a temperature, she felt her forehead to see if maybe she was the one who was sick and imagining that the kids wanted to go to sleep.

"Titus, does that fact that all of you want to go to sleep have anything to do with the dream you told me about this morning? You know that Dreamland is not real, right?" Mrs. Drapkin said.

Titus told his mom that it seems very real for kids. Grownups are too old to go to the kid part of Dreamland unless they are invited, so that is why she didn't think it was real.

"Well, that is not entirely true. When I was your age, I used to go to Dreamland from time to time," said Mrs. Drapkin.

"But without stuffed animal hosts like Harper and Remy, you can't visit the parts of Dreamland we go to," Titus pointed out.

"If that is the case, then I think you should try to keep a dream journal by your bed; as soon as you wake up each morning, you can write down your dreams. This way, I can have a better understanding of Dreamland, and you can remember where to start your next dream," explained Mrs. Drapkin.

Titus and Constance thought that a dream journal was a good idea. They promised to write in it every morning after they had a dream. They each got a pencil and pad to put next to their beds, hugged their mom and dad, placed Harper and Remy in their matchboxes and closed their eyes so they could pick up the dream where they had left off.

CHAPTER 6

The Train Ride

Within minutes of falling asleep, Titus appeared back in the sleeper car in the same cowboy outfit he had on the night before. Soon, both Constance and Evie showed up too. Titus forgot to tell Constance that she should dream which clothes she wanted to wear for the trip, so Constance showed up in her pink nightgown with her white furry slippers, and Evie was in her red onesie sleeper, carrying her stuffed hamster doll, Mr. Hamster.

"Titus, I am glad you are back," said Harper. "The mayor is in the dining car, waiting for us." Harper looked at Constance and Evie and said, "Welcome back. You are just in time for a new adventure. Titus, how come you didn't tell Constance about dressing up for the train trip? We can't take her to the dining car in a nighty and slippers."

Since there wasn't a store on the train, the only option was to have Constance and Evie dream up clothes now.

"Constance, Evie, can you remember the dresses you got last Easter?" asked Remy. "Can you imagine you and Evie dressed up like that so we can go to dinner?"

The two girls closed their eyes and imagined their Easter dresses. Instantly, Constance was wearing her white dress with blue violets printed on it, her white dress shoes and her white straw hat with a purple ribbon. Evie's onesie turned into her yellow dress with a white ribbon and matching yellow slip-on shoes. Titus stayed dressed in his cowboy outfit since it was his dream, and he had no desire to wear his Sunday blue suit, white shirt and tie if he didn't have to.

All three of the kids, led by Harper and Remy, made their way through the train to the dining car. They passed by lots of other sleeper cars. They saw cars with people sitting on benches, a car with games and a library and an observation car. After walking for a long time, they finally got to the dining car. The mayor was sitting by the window with a napkin around his neck and a fork and knife in his hands.

"Harper, it is about time you got here. I am starving and can't wait to eat. I see you brought Titus, Remy, Constance and little Evie," said the mayor.

"Yes," said Harper, "it is sleeping time in the real world, so everyone decided to join us for our trip to Willets. Is that okay with you?"

"Sure, there should be enough room in the sleeper car for everyone," the mayor said.

"Excuse me, Mayor," said Titus, "but I am traveling to Dreamland for adventure, not to sleep. I can sleep at home." Mayor Downing let out a loud laugh, and soon Harper and Remy were laughing too.

"Titus, I am sorry. I wasn't laughing at you, but keep in mind this is your dream, so you don't have to do anything you don't want to. Now, let's eat," the mayor said while still chuckling.

In no time, waiters dressed in white coats with black bow ties and shiny black shoes were bringing food to the table. There was a plate full of roast turkey and bowls of stuffing, creamed string beans, rolls, mashed potatoes, gravy and cranberry sauce.

"Well, I didn't dream this meal up, but if I had, the only difference I would make is that there would be no string beans. Oh, and I'd make sure there was a hot apple pie and pumpkin pie with whipped cream for dessert," Titus blurted out, his mouth full of stuffing.

"As you know, vegetables are good for you, so if you eat the string beans, I will make sure the desserts follow the meal," said the mayor between mouthfuls of food.

After everyone ate all the food they wanted, and when they had finished their two pieces of pie, they went to the observation car to watch the scenery go by. Remy acted as a tour guide.

"On your right is Mount Pleasant, the tallest mountain on the west coast of Dreamland. Notice it has snow at the top," Remy lectured.

"Remy, have you ever climbed to the top?" asked Constance.

"Yes," said Remy. "If you start at the beginning of a dream, you can reach the top before you wake up. It is quite an adventure since there are waterfalls, streams and many caves to explore along the way. Most kids make it a two-dream adventure. And on a clear day, you can see all the way to Sanderling Island."

Evie left the group and walked to the other side of the observation car to watch the sunset. Soon, the whole group was over on that side watching the sunset. "How long will it take to get to Willets?" asked Evie.

"It usually takes two days, but if you are in a hurry, just think about pulling into the station and we will be there," said the mayor. Titus was tempted to do that, but he was also enjoying the train ride. After all, how many times do you get to ride on a vintage train?

"I am enjoying myself on the train, so I think I will explore it before we get to Willets. How about I meet you all back in the sleeper car a little later," stated Titus.

By this time, everyone was sitting at a small round table in the observation car enjoying jasmine mint tea and butter cookies while watching the sunset, so Titus took a couple of cookies, put them in his vest pocket and headed toward the front of the train.

He passed back through the dining car where the waiters were cleaning up after dinner, then he walked through the kitchen car with its large refrigerators, sinks and ovens and entered the mail car. Inside the mail car were a few cages with the oddest-looking creatures he had ever seen. They were about two feet tall with blue fur, four legs, a long tail and huge large blue eyes and ears.

Knowing that nothing could hurt him in Dreamland, Titus went up to the biggest creature and said hello. To his surprise, the creature could speak. "Hi, my name is Milo. What is your name?"

"My name is Titus. What are you, and where do you come from?" asked Titus.

The creature responded, "I am a kumon from Ronsdale Village, south of Ploverville. It is the southernmost village on the west coast of Dreamland."

"So why are you in a cage?" asked Titus.

"kumons are house pets for Dreamlanders," stated Milo.

"So, you would be kind of a cross between a cat and dog from where I come from, but our pets can't speak," Titus said.

"That's odd," Milo said. "How do they communicate with you?"

"Through meows, barking or movement," said Titus. "I think it would be great to have a pet that could talk," Titus went on to say. "I plan on doing a lot of traveling in Dreamland. Maybe I will make a trip down to Ronsdale to visit your village."

51

"If you do," Milo said, "stop by the firehouse and ask for Chief Barron. He is also our mayor and will be happy to show you around."

"Where are you heading to?" Titus asked Milo.

"My owner is taking me to Willets to visit her relatives. We will be at Willets for a week and then head home," said Milo. "She is the squirrel wearing a pretty velvet blue dress and a white hat with acorns around the top. Her name is Myra, and she is staying in one of the sleeper cars with her children. Maybe you will see her when we all get off the train," Mio added.

"It was nice meeting you, Milo. I am heading towards the engine, so maybe I will see you again on my way back to my sleeper car."

When Titus got to the engine, he noticed the engineer and conductor shouting and pointing at the tracks ahead. Titus looked out at the tracks and saw a large log laying across the tracks. He also saw some badgers dressed in cowboy outfits hiding behind trees on either side of the tracks.

Titus shouted to the train engineer, "Don't stop! I think this is a holdup. You should speed up and ram the log."

Apparently, the engineer and conductor both had the same idea. The engineer sped the train up, and within seconds, there was a loud noise, and the train shook all over.

It turns out the shaking was not caused by the train, but by his mother trying to wake him.

"Titus, its time to wake up," his mother said.

Titus was again not happy to be so rudely awoken from a great dream. He went into Constance's room to see if she was awake and noticed she was writing in her dream journal. He forgot all about his dream journal, so he quickly wrote down what he remembered and then got dressed for breakfast.

During breakfast, Titus told Constance about the badgers, and Constance told Titus about the game they all played in the sleeper car. As it turns out, Evie beat them all. Three times!

As much as Titus, Constance and Evie all liked the train, they couldn't wait until they got to Willets. Titus suggested to Constance that tonight, they dream about being in the sleeper car as they pull into the train station.

"This way we avoid the badgers, and we don't have to spend any time in Dreamland sleeping."

Constance thought that was a good idea.

After the bedtime story that night, all three kids went to sleep quickly to dream about adventures in Willets.

CHAPTER 7

Willets

Evie was the first to arrive back in the sleeper car. She brought Mr. Hamster with her, and she was dressed for walking around the village. Harper, Remy and the mayor had just finished packing.

"The train will be pulling into the station any minute. Where are Titus and Constance?" asked the mayor.

"They should be here shortly," Evie said. "I could hear Titus snoring."

Right as she said this, Titus and Constance appeared in the sleeper car ready for action. Titus was still wearing his cowboy outfit, and this time, Constance had on a bright red cowgirl skirt, brown and red boots, a red and white shirt with a red vest and a matching red hat. Evie took one look at Constance's outfit, clicked her heels together three times and was instantly wearing the same outfit as Constance, only her outfit was in blue.

The mayor asked the porter if he could store the luggage at the train station while they went into town, and the porter agreed. As he was taking the luggage from the room, the mayor tipped the porter 20 acorns, which was the currency of Willets.

As they left the train, Titus noticed that Willets was nothing more than an old cowboy town, like the ones from the westerns he read about in his dime novels his dad would take home from the store.

The station was a weathered wooden building with a small waiting room that had benches in the center. Inside was also a ticket office and a telegraph office. Once they walked through the waiting room, they stepped down to a dirt street that ran the length of the town.

Walking up and down the street, Titus noticed that the town's squirrels were dressed in cowboy outfits, fancy dresses or three-piece suits. "Looks like we wore the right clothes for this dream!" exclaimed Titus. Most of the town squirrels kept their distance from Titus, Constance and Evie and gave dirty looks to Harper, Remy and the mayor. It seems word got out that the mayor was in town to collect money and the squirrel clan wasn't very happy about it.

The sheriff walked from the jail to where the group was standing. He stuck out his hand and said, "I am Sheriff Tanner." The sheriff was tall for a squirrel. He also seemed kind of old for the job. He wore a brown vest with a silver star, and a brown cowboy hat, and he had a gun holstered on his waist. "I see you brought three gunslingers with you to collect the money," said the sheriff, in a deep voice. "We don't want any trouble, so have your hired gunslingers hand over their guns."

Titus forgot that when they all dreamt up cowboy outfits this time, they included toy guns and holsters. Titus was about to tell the Sheriff that the guns were toys, but Mayor Downing, sensing trouble, told the sheriff, "There shouldn't be any gunplay since we are just here to collect the money that Mayor Bushytail already agreed to pay. There is no reason for my gunslingers to hand over their guns as there should be no trouble."

Titus looked over at the mayor wondering what he was talking about when he saw the mayor give him a sly wink. Titus whispered in Constance and Evie's ear to just play along and look mean.

The sheriff took a step back since he wasn't used to people not following his directions. "Well," said the sheriff, "the townsfolk had a meeting last night in the town hall, and they decided that the youngster squirrel knocked over the cart by accident, so they should not have to pay for the roasted nuts that fell on the ground."

The sheriff crossed his arms and nodded to the barn behind them. "As a matter of fact, just on the other side of that barn is a band of armed squirrels ready to come here and shoot it out if I give them the order."

Constance didn't like the direction this was going. After all, they only had toy guns, and they didn't really want to shoot it out over some spilled nuts.

"Excuse me, Sheriff," Constance said in her best western voice, "we have traveled a long way to get here, and we don't want any trouble.

Maybe if we talk to Mayor Bushytail, we can work this out without anyone getting hurt."

This surprised the sheriff, coming from what he thought was a professional gunslinger. He started getting concerned that maybe his townsfolk would not be a match for the three hired hands. "Okay, let's go over to the mayor's office, but I am going to keep my eye on you three to make sure there is no funny business."

As they walked to the mayor's office, Titus, Constance and Evie all strutted like the mean outlaws they had seen in the silent films shown at the small theater back in their town. They tilted their hats forward, squinted their eyes, took slow but long steps and hovered their hands over their guns like they were ready to draw at any second. Behind them followed Mayor Downing, Harper and Remy, all trying hard not to laugh.

Everyone cleared out of the group's way as they made their way down the center of the street. Squirrel children hid behind their mother's skirts, and even the stray kumons ran under the wooden sidewalks that lined each side of the street to hide in case there was gunplay.

When they arrived at Mayor Bushytail's office, the sheriff, Harper, Remy and Mayor Downing went in first and Titus and Constance followed. Evie stayed outside to guard the door, holding Mr. Hamster by her side. The mayor's office was small and dark. It had a wooden plank floor, with a worn-out carpet in the center, a potbelly stove, several bookshelves filled with legal books and a large mahogany desk with three padded chairs in front. Sitting behind the desk was Mayor Bushytail. Titus remembered the stuffed animal he found in the barn and noticed the mayor had added a few pounds and his fur had a lot more gray.

Harper, Remy and Mayor Downing sat down in the chairs while Constance and Titus stood behind them. Mayor Downing spoke first. Instead of the usual friendly greetings and small talk about the weather and the townsfolk, Mayor Downing got right to the point. "What's this? I hear that you don't want to pay for the spilled nuts?"

"Well," Mayor Bushytail spurted out, "it wasn't me that changed my mind. It was the townsfolk. They felt they shouldn't have to pay since it was an accident."

"Did you tell them we had an agreement?" Mayor Downing questioned. "After all, when you make an agreement, you should stick to it. Your word is one of the most important character traits you possess. If it gets out you broke an agreement, no one will trust you in the future," lectured Mayor Downing.

Mayor Bushytail thought for a moment. Mayor Downing did have a good point that he had not considered when he agreed with the townsfolk not to pay. Now he had to make a decision: he could honor his agreement with Puffin Village, or he could side with his townsfolk. Titus could see Mayor Bushytail was stuck between two hard decisions. Titus thought of a way to help the mayor out of the mess he was in.

"Excuse me, Mayor Bushytail, do you remember a real-worlder named Jack who was here many years ago?" asked Titus.

"Why, yes. Jack and I were great friends. As a matter of fact, I was his animal host for Dreamland. We went on some great adventures back then," the mayor said with a tender smile.

"Well, Jack is my dad and he is also Constance and Evie's dad too."

Mayor Bushytail looked shocked. "If he is your dad, why would he send you gunslingers to Willets to help out Puffin Village?" inquired the mayor.

Titus laughed. "We aren't gunslingers! These are toy guns, and these are just outfits we dreamed up for the trip." At that point, everyone laughed, even the sheriff. This removed all of the tension in the room.

Mayor Bushytail now saw a way out of his dilemma. "That changes everything," said the mayor. "Once the townsfolk know you are the children of Jack, they will agree to pay for the spilled nuts and probably even throw a party for you since everyone in the village, old enough to remember Jack, thought he was a great guy."

Mayor Busytail told the sheriff to get everyone to the town hall for an announcement he was going to give. After the sheriff left to assemble the squirrel clan in the town hall, Mayor Bushytail apologized to Mayor Downing for the unfriendly reception they received when they arrived and for trying to break the agreement. Mayor Downing said he understood how peer pressure can make you do things you know are not right. "It is a lot easier to follow the crowd than to stand up against it," said Mayor Downing in an understanding voice.

Mayor Bushytail asked the group if they could stay for a while and come to the town picnic they were planning later in the day. Titus told him he and his siblings could stay until they had to wake up from the dream, and Harper, Remy and Mayor Downing said their return train trip wasn't scheduled until tomorrow afternoon so they could attend as well.

The mayor stood up, went over to the safe and took out a large canvas bag with a string tied around the top. "Here is the money we owe," said the mayor.

Mayor Downing gave it back to him and asked, "Could you keep it in the safe tonight for safe keeping? I will pick it up tomorrow when we leave."

Mayor Bushytail put it back in the safe, closed the door and spun the dial to lock the safe.

"That's the least I can do for all the problems we have caused," said Mayor Bushytail. "Let's all head over to the town hall so I can make the announcement."

Everyone followed Mayor Bushytail over to the town hall. They entered a side door that was up a flight of wooden stairs. Once they entered the hall, they found themselves on stage with all of the squirrel clan staring at them. In the back of the room were a few squirrels holding rifles just in case they didn't like what the mayor said.

"Squirrel clan, please quiet down. The mayor has an announcement to make," yelled the sheriff over the noise of the crowd.

Soon, the hall was quiet, and the mayor stepped up to the podium. "Ladies and gentle squirrels, as we all know, one of our own clan knocked over the nut roasting cart when he was in Puffin Village, destroying all the nuts. Instead of doing the honorable thing by going up to the owner and apologizing, he and his friends ran out of town," the mayor exclaimed. "This does not represent the true character of Willets " The mayor cleared his throat. "Last night, most of the townsfolk protested against paying for the damages, claiming it had been an accident, and at that time, I agreed." The mayor added, "That was a wrong decision since I had already agreed to pay Puffin Village."

At this point, a loud murmur began to build in the crowd. Someone yelled out, "But you agreed with us that you weren't going to pay, so which agreement are you going to break?"

"The agreement I made to Puffin Village was the first agreement while the one I made to the clan was the second agreement, and we

61

need to honor the first agreement made," the mayor stated. "With one agreement in place, I should not have made a second agreement. It was not the honorable or neighborly thing to do," the mayor added.

"Well, sending three hired gunslingers to collect the money isn't very neighborly either," shouted one of the gunmen in the back of the room.

The mayor said laughingly, "These aren't gunslingers. These are the children of Jack, my real-world friend I used to go on adventures with years ago."

A rather rotund lady squirrel in the front row declared, "I remember Jack! He used to come to my house for milk and cookies. You all look just like him," she said with a big smile on her face.

Soon, many of the other clan squirrels started yelling that they remembered Jack and one added, "Well, that changes things. Since they aren't gunslingers, and they are relatives of Jack, we should honor our initial agreement." Shortly, the whole crowd was in agreement. The men in the back laid down their guns and everyone started forming a line to walk on stage and greet Titus, Constance, Evie, Harper, Remy and Mayor Downing.

The greeting line seemed to go on forever. Fortunately, the lady in the front, whom everyone called Grandma K, yelled out in a surprisingly loud voice, which was heard over the noise of the crowd, "Hey everyone, enough of this! Let's go to the picnic."

Everyone cheered and began filing out the front door, making their way towards the picnic grounds.

Harper and Remy were as relieved as Titus, Constance and Evie to end the greeting line and get to the picnic. Titus couldn't wait to see all of the food they had laid out on the tables and Constance couldn't wait to hear more stories about their dad. Evie had to go to the bathroom, so she started crying to wake up her mother. Before Titus could stop her, all three were back in their beds at home.

"Rats!" yelled Titus so loud that Constance could hear him from her room. Each of the older kids got their dream journals out and made detailed notes so they could return to the picnic that night.

CHAPTER 8

The Picnic

At dinner that evening, Jack asked Titus and Constance if they had any interesting dreams the night before. Titus had been waiting all day to tell his father about their adventure in Willets, but as he started to tell the story, he realized he already forgot most of the dream. Constance jumped up from her seat, and as she was running for her room, she could be heard yelling, "Good thing we keep a dream journal!"

When she returned, she told her parents about their trip to Willets, the gunfight they almost had on Main Street, their meeting Sheriff Tanner and the Mayor Bushytail, the town hall meeting, Grandma K and the picnic they were hoping to go to tonight when they returned to Dreamland. Jack said that now that Constance reminded him, he remembered Sheriff Tanner and how he and Squirrely went over to Grandma K's house for milk and cookies on occasion.

Titus asked his dad if he ever went to the picnic when he was in Willets. Jack nodded and let out a laugh saying that it reminded him of a story.

"One day, I arrived in Willets when they were still setting up for the picnic. Squirrely thought it would be fun to steal a pie and take it to the forest to eat it since we were hungry and didn't want to wait to eat, much less wait for dessert."

Jack shook his head, "I tried to stop Squirrely since we all know it is not right to steal, but it was too late. Squirrely had climbed a tree and crawled out on a limb that hung over the table. When he thought no one was looking, he dropped to the ground and crawled under the tablecloth. From where I was standing, I could see Squirrely reach his furry little arm from under the tablecloth and grab a pecan pie. I saw Sheriff Tanner walking towards the table. I tried to warn Squirrely by yelling hi to Sheriff Tanner with my outside voice. Just as Sheriff Tanner turned around to see who was greeting him, Squirrely lost his grip on the pie and it fell right on his head, its filling spilling all over Squirrely.

"Grandma K, who had spent hours preparing the pie, gave a short scream and fainted right on the grass. Sheriff Tanner soon figured out what was happening and yelled at us to go to the jail and wait for him while he attended to Grandma K.

"Squirrely and I knew we were in trouble. On the way over to the jail, Squirrely was trying out all kinds of stories he could tell the sheriff to get out of trouble. 'How about saying that I was walking by the pie table and when you yelled hi to the sheriff, I tripped and knocked over the pie,' Squirrely said.

"'How does that explain the pie landing on your head?'

"'Good point,' said Squirrely, scratching his head. 'I didn't think about that. Okay, how about I was up in the tree and when you yelled hi, I fell down and landed face first in the pie?'

"I gave Squirrely a look. 'How about we tell the truth,' I said. 'First off, you know you should never lie. Second, when you lie, you are constantly overlooking something, and at some point, the truth will come out and you will be in more trouble. Plus, people won't trust you anymore.'

"After about 10 minutes, the sheriff showed up and told us to take a seat in front of his desk. 'Now tell me what happened,' he said in a very menacing voice.

"Squirrely started out, 'Well you see Sheriff, I was walking by' I gave Squirrely a hard kick in the leg under the table. He gave me a dirty look since he couldn't yell, then continued, 'Well Sheriff, the truth is that I was hungry, and I didn't want to wait for the picnic to start, so I thought since there were so many pies, if I took one, no one would notice it was gone. Jack told me not to do it, and I think he was trying to distract you by yelling hi so I wouldn't get in trouble.'

"'Is that true, Jack?' asked the sheriff.

"'Yes,' I responded.

"'Okay,' said the sheriff, 'usually in this case, since you are so young, I would tell your parents and let them punish you. But since you

66

told the truth, I won't tell your parents, and your punishment will be to sweep out the jail and take out the garbage.' Both of us were relieved. I took out the garbage while Squirrely swept out all the jail cells and the sheriff's office.

"'How is Grandma K?' I asked the Sheriff.

"'She is fine since she landed on the soft grass, but she is not happy about the pie.'

"'What are you going to tell her about what happened to the pie?' asked Squirrely.

"'No, what are *you* going to tell her,' the Sheriff responded.

"'Well,' Squirrely paused. 'I'll tell her the truth, and that I've learned my lesson. From now on, I will not steal and I will not lie.'

"'If you keep that up, maybe someday you can be Mayor of Willets,' the sheriff said with a playful smile.

"By the time we finished cleaning the jail, the picnic was over, and I woke up for school, so we missed the picnic altogether."

That evening after dinner, Jack announced, "Now it's time for you guys to get ready for bed." Thirty minutes later, everything was cleaned up from dinner, the kids all had their baths and they were in bed ready to go back to Willets for the picnic.

Harper and Remy were waiting for them by the same tree Squirrely (Mayor Bushytail) had used to try and steal the pie. Soon, all three of the kids were back, dressed in the same outfits, but this time they left the guns and holsters out of the dream. Mayor Downing was talking to Mayor Bushytail, and the sheriff was walking over to speak with Harper, Remy and the kids. Titus greeted the sheriff and asked him if he remembered the time that Squirrely and his dad almost took the pie.

"Yes," said the sheriff. "They actually tell the story in school to the young squirrels as a lesson in honesty. As a matter of fact, it helped Squirrely, I mean Mayor Bushytail, get elected as mayor."

"That sounds like our story about George Washington cutting down the cherry tree," said Constance.

"I knew George when he was a young boy, and I really doubt he would have cut down the tree," said the sheriff.

"Wow!" exclaimed Titus, "You knew George Washington when he was young?"

"Yes," responded the sheriff. "Grandma K was his Dreamland animal host. She knows all kinds of stories about him." The sheriff sighed, "Back then, kids had to grow up fast, so he was only in Dreamland for a short time."

"I'm hungry," said Evie.

"Looks like things are ready for the picnic. Let's head over to hear the mayor's speech, which he gives before each picnic can start," said Remy.

As the mayor climbed up the stairs to the gazebo to start his speech, Evie clicked her heels together three times and wished the speech would be short.

The mayor opened his mouth and said, "Let's eat," and climbed back down the stairs.

The surprised sheriff said, "That was the shortest speech the mayor has ever given! Come on now, let's all get in line." Evie giggled to herself and was the first person in line.

Titus could not believe his eyes. There was fried chicken, BBQ ribs, hot dogs, hamburgers, corn on the cob, bean salad, potato salad and all kinds of vegetables to eat. On another table, there were pies, cookies, and brownies, and at the end of the table, Deputy Don was turning a large handle to make fresh vanilla ice cream.

After everyone stuffed themselves, Mayor Downing reminded them that they had a train to catch in a few hours to head back to Puffin Village. Titus asked if Harper and he could stop at the train station at Mount Pleasant to go on an adventure before returning to Puffin Village. The mayor said that would be fine. Constance and Evie wanted to spend more time in Willets to explore and hear stories about George Washington and their dad from Grandma K, so she asked the mayor if it would be okay if she, Remy and Evie stayed in Willets a little longer, and the mayor agreed to that too. It seems that Mayor Downing had a lot of documents to read, so he thought having time to himself on the ride back was a good idea.

Mayor Downing walked over to the table where Mayor Bushytail was sitting and reminded him he had a train to catch in a few hours, so they both took off to the mayor's office to collect the bag of money. While he was doing this, Sheriff Tanner walked Harper, Remy and the three children around and introduced them to the squirrel clan. When they got to the table where Grandma K was sitting, she insisted that everyone sit down and join her.

"I remember when your dad was your age, Titus," Grandma K started. "He and Mayor Bushytail were quite the little troublemakers. One day, when they came by for milk and cookies, your dad pulled a frog out of his pocket to show me, and I screamed so loud the frog jumped up and fell down the back of my dress. I was dancing around the room trying to get the frog out while your dad and Mayor Bushytail were on the floor laughing so hard they could barely catch their breaths. Finally, I loosened my belt, and the frog fell on the floor. I grabbed the broom and first shooed the frog out of the house and then I went after the two boys. Because they were laughing so hard, I was able to swat them several times before your dad disappeared back to the real-world and before the mayor went running out of the house, still laughing and stumbling as he ran. Now that I think about it, it must have been quite a sight to see me dancing around the room!" All three of the kids started laughing, and soon they disappeared too.

"Well," said Harper, "looks like they must be awake. Hopefully, they will join us tonight when they go back to sleep."

CHAPTER 9

The Acorn Arcade

When everyone returned to Dreamland that night, Harper, Titus and Mayor Downing were on the train to Mount Pleasant and Puffin Village, and Constance, Remy and Evie were at Grandma K's house having milk and cookies. "This is the same table your dad used to sit at when he was here," said Grandma K.

"Do you remember any more stories about my dad?" asked Constance.

Grandma K thought for a moment. "One day, when your dad and the Mayor were hiking in the hills above the town, they came across an old abandoned cabin. Everyone just called the mayor Squirrely back then. Squirrely, being the more adventurous of the two, suggested they go in and check out the cabin. What your dad didn't know was that Squirrely was a practical joker, and Sheriff Tanner and Deputy Dan, who were just called Tanner and Dan back then, were hiding in the cabin waiting for Squirrely to bring your dad in."

"Then what happened?" Evie asked impatiently.

"When Squirrely and your dad entered the cabin, it was dark and smelled of old fires from the potbelly stove and damp wooden floors. Your dad, always hungry like Titus, went right over to the large cupboard to see if there was any food. As soon as he opened it, Tanner jumped out and yelled surprise. Your dad was so surprised that he stepped back and tripped over the bear rug on the floor. Dan was hiding under the rug, and as soon as your dad fell down, Dan stood up with the bear rug wrapped around him and the bear's head over his head. He roared at the top of his lungs. Your dad went running out of the cabin so fast that he tripped over a branch and slid down the hill right into the pond. When your dad looked up, Squirrely, Tanner and Don were all standing by the pond laughing so hard, that he was able to get out of the pond and pull them all in with him. They all sat there laughing until your dad woke up and disappeared. This started a series of practical jokes that went back and forth between Squirrely and your dad for years," Grandma K said chuckling the whole time she was telling the story.

Constance and Evie both laughed as they pictured their dad being scared and falling into the pond. Remy laughed too.

"Can you tell us a story about George Washington?" asked Constance.

"That was almost two hundred years ago," Grandma K said in deep thought. "Let me think now." She paused for another brief moment. "George was only here for a short time. His father died when he was only eleven, and he never came back after that. It wasn't that he

72

couldn't come back, but he had to take on so many responsibilities to help his mother, that he grew up too fast. George loved math and spelling, so when he was here, he would sometimes help Ms. Karen, the school teacher, with lessons at our local school," Grandma K added.

"Why would anyone want to go to school while they were in Dreamland, much less help teach math and spelling?" asked Constance.

"If you knew George like I did, you would know that he loved to help other people so much that he dreamt about it," responded Grandma K.

Evie, being too young to know who George Washington was, was getting restless to see more of Willets. She was about to click her heels together when there was a knock on the door. Grandma K opened the door and standing there was a shy small squirrel dressed in white shorts, a white and blue striped shirt and holding a boy's sailor cap in his hands.

"Hi," the boy said. "I am Josh and my father, Sheriff Tanner, told me to come over and help show you around Willets."

Evie jumped up and ran over to the door wondering to herself if she dreamed Josh up without clicking her heels or if Josh just showed up at the nick of time to rescue her.

"Hi, I am Evie," she said with a wave. "It is nice seeing someone my size. How old are you?"

"I am four years old in real-world time," he said.

While Josh and Evie were becoming friends, Constance and Remy helped Grandma K clear the table. "Come back any time you are in Willets," said Grandma K. "I would love to hear how your dad turned out. Maybe you can bring him back with you one of these times."

"I thought older people couldn't come to this part of Dreamland," Constance said.

"Well, if he still has his Dreamland animal, and if he can clear his mind of all the clutter he has put in it over the years, he should be able to make the trip back."

Everyone said their goodbyes to Grandma K, and they all headed up Main Street to the center of town. "What would you like to do first?" asked Josh.

"I want to go on an adventure," Evie quickly stated.

"Sometimes, a lot of the squirrel clan kids likes to sneak into the old abandoned firehouse at the end of the street," Josh said. "They climb up to the top of the bell tower, which was used to spot fires and warn the squirrel clan by ringing the bell."

"Sneaking, doesn't sound like something we should do," said Constance.

"You are right," said Josh. "I used the wrong word. Everyone is allowed to go in, it just sounds more like an adventure if it is something you aren't supposed to do."

"Let's go," said Evie.

"I have never been to the old fire station," added Remy. "it sounds like fun."

The front door to the abandoned firehouse was locked, so they all walked around the side, past tumbleweeds and thorn bushes. The side door was opening and closing with the wind.

"Are you sure this place isn't haunted?" Evie asked, having second thoughts. She hugged her Mr. Hamster doll to her chest and had a concerned look on her face. Remy reminded her that in this part of Dreamland, there were no bad things or things that could hurt or scare her.

Josh went through the door first, followed by Remy and Constance. Evie came in once Constance told her it was all clear. Josh led them to an old rickety staircase and started climbing up. With every step, the boards let out a loud creak, almost as if they were going to break. The staircase wound around the side of the bell tower, so it took quite a long time and a bit of effort to get up to the top. The bell was moved years ago to the new firehouse so the only thing left was an old rope, some spiderwebs and a family of owls.

"Hey, kids," the owl mom whispered to her little owls. "Wake up, it looks like we have company." All the little owls opened their large eyes and stared at Evie and Constance. The young owls were too little to ever remember any real-world people coming to their home.

Evie whispered to Constance, "Did you hear those owls talk, or are they just talking in my dream?" Remy overheard Evie and told them that all of the animals in Dreamland can talk if they want to.

"Mama Owl, I would like to introduce you to my friends from the real-world." Josh motioned to the girls. "This is Constance and the little one is Evie. And this is Remy from Puffin Village," announced Josh.

"Pleasure to meet you," said Mama Owl. "This is Brownie, this is Feathers, and hiding under my wing is little Furball." Little Furball stuck his head out for a second to see the people and then went back under his mother's wing.

"What part of the real-world are you from?" asked Mama Owl.

"We are from Idaho," answered Constance. "It is beautiful with warm summers and snowy winters."

"Sounds nice," said Mama Owl. "Do you have worms in Idaho?" she asked.

"Yes, big juicy ones," Constance responded. Mama Owl's big eyes got even larger when Constance mentioned the juicy worms. Evie wrinkled her nose just thinking about big juicy worms.

"Remy, have you been to Willets before?" asked Mama Owl.

"Yes, but as I was telling Josh, I have never been up in the old firehouse tower before. You can see all of Willets from up here," Remy added.

"Let me act as your guide," responded Mama Owl.

Mama Owl shooed Furball out from under her wing, and Furball hopped behind Feathers to hide. Mama Owl flew out of the bell tower and hoovered as she used her beak to point out places of interest in Willets. "To your left is the train station; past that is the horse corral, blacksmith, and barn. Next to that is the candle shop, candy store, and bakery. Behind me are the sheriff's office and jail. Near that are the hotel, restaurant and the mayor's office. Way down at the far end is the park and the fairgrounds."

Mama Owl flew to the opposite side of the bell tower and the others followed, making sure they could see the rest of the town. Mama Owl went on, "Near the fairgrounds is where most of the Squirrel clan lives, and that house is where Grandma K lives. Next to those is the new firehouse and the church, and behind the church on the hill is the schoolhouse." Mama Owl turned around to see if everyone was following. "In the middle of town is our new theater and general store, and that large building is the Acorn Arcade. Finally, that big house is where Mayor Bushytail lives."

Josh thanked Mama Owl for the tour and suggested that the group head down the stairs and make their way towards the arcade as it was

77

brand new and the biggest attraction in Willets. Everyone said goodbye to the Owl family and started heading downstairs.

The Acorn Arcade was a two-story magnificent building with a large sign reading "Mr. Nut's Acorn Arcade" across the top of the building. As they entered, they saw a large hall with an arched stained-glass ceiling that was two stories high and ran the length of the building. Along the sides on both the ground and second-story floors were all kinds of games to play. There were even moving picture machines that you could watch for one acorn.

Remy was very impressed because they didn't have anything like this back in Puffin Village. Constance and Evie had been to the new arcade in Boise, Idaho, but it was not nearly as big nor beautiful as this. Mr. Nut's Acorn Arcade looked more like the photos of the fancy arcades in New York City.

Knowing that she and Evie were coming back to Willets and that acorns were their currency, Constance had remembered to dream up a purse full of acorns to take with her in case an opportunity like this arose.

As they walked around the arcade, they saw games with metal guns to shoot at targets and games of strength where you squeeze a handle and a light tells you how strong you are. They also saw a mechanical piano that played a song for an acorn.

Towards the back of the arcade, they saw a fortune teller game. Inside was a man with a turban on his head; he was looking into a crystal ball.

"Let's try hearing what the fortune teller has to say," said Evie. The whole group gathered around the fortune teller, and Constance opened her purse to get an acorn to put into the machine. After she deposited the acorn, the head lifted up, the hands waved over the crystal ball, and the fortune teller started to speak.

"I see many adventures in your future," the fortune teller announced in a deep mechanical voice. "You will visit many lands and meet the inhabitants of each land. I also see your mother coming into your room and waking you up for breakfast."

"Huh?" Evie started to say. "How docs he know that?" The next thing Evie saw was her mother leaving her room to go wake Constance up.

CHAPTER 10

Mount Pleasant

That evening, Constance brought her dream journal to the dinner table to tell the family about the wonderful adventure she and Evie had in Willets. She told them about going to Grandma K's house for milk and cookies, about the story of George Washington when he was a boy and about the practical joke that Squirrely, Tanner and Don had played on their dad.

Jack had completely forgotten about that story. He laughed and said that was the first of many jokes they played on each other over the years. "Boy, those were fun times," Jack said. Constance told her dad that Grandma K wished he would come back for a visit and how Harper said he may be able to do so if he sleeps with his old squirrel stuffed animal near him. "I may just try that one night. It would be great to go back to see the old gang," said Jack.

Constance continued telling them about meeting Josh, the son of Sheriff Tanner, and about how Evie and Josh became friends. Before Constance could tell about the Owl family and the arcade, Titus had returned from his room with his dream journal and started to tell about his dream.

Titus told them that after Mayor Downing, he and Harper collected the suitcases from the porter and loaded them into the same sleeper car they went to Willets in, they had a great dinner and then watched the scenery in the observation car. Harper pointed out all the points of interest and said, "We can have many adventures just between Puffin Village and Willets."

Tyler continued with his story. "In no time, the train pulled into Mount Pleasant train station, and Harper and I said our goodbyes to the mayor and departed the train. It was still early morning, so we had a lot of time to hike the mountain before sunset."

He paused to take another bite of his dinner. "The train station was nothing more than a wooden platform with sheets of rusty metal running the length of the platform to provide protection from the rain and sun. There was one long wooden bench in the center. As we stepped down from the platform, hundreds of the oddest-looking rabbits surrounded us. The strange rabbits were slim with necks so long that when they were sitting, they were the same height as Harper and I. All of a sudden, and at the same time, they raised a paw over their heads and yelled, 'Pick me, pick me.' I turned to Harper and asked him what these creatures were and what they wanted to be picked for. Harper told me they were babbits, and they were guides for Mount Pleasant.

"I started asking Harper what we needed guides for when a large babbit made his way through the crowd and came up to Harper and

81

gave him a big hug. 'Harper, my old friend,' the babbit shouted. 'What a pleasant surprise. How long has it been?'

"'Tyler, I would like you to meet Titus, he is my new friend from the real-world.'

"'Oh, what part?' asked Tyler.

"'Idaho,' I responded.

"'I've heard that is a nice place,' Tyler said.

"Tyler asked us if we were going to climb Mount Pleasant today, and Harper told him yes.

"'Well, let's get started,' Tyler said and he made his way through the crowd of babbits. We followed him. Tyler picked out two of the babbits, Zoe and Coker, to carry our backpacks that Harper had ready for our trip. They were filled with snacks, water and some supplies. I commented to Tyler that the backpacks were too heavy for the babbits and we could carry them on our own, but he would hear none of it. Later, Harper told me that this is what the babbits live for, and we would be hurting their feelings if we didn't let them carry our supplies."

At this point, the family was finished having dinner, and Mrs. Drapkin suggested that the kids get ready for bed and that Titus could tell the rest of the story instead of having a story read to them.

The kids did everything they needed to get ready for bed, and while Titus was brushing his teeth, Constance and Evie were in Titus's bed where they usually all heard a bedtime story, with their dad reading and their mom sitting on the end of the bed. Constance told her dad about the large arcade they were in and the fortune teller. Jack remembered the arcade and started telling a story about the time he and Squirrely found a large bag of acorns in a field one day and spent the entire day in the arcade playing games with those acorns.

Just then, Titus came into the room with his dream journal, climbed in the center of the bed with Evie on one side and Constance on the other and said, "Okay, where were we?" After flipping through some of the pages, he said, "This is where I left off. We set off up a narrow trail that leads to the top of Mount Pleasant with Tyler in the lead and Harper behind him. I trailed behind Harper. Following my lead were the two little babbits, huffing and puffing from carrying our backpacks.

"Our first challenge was to get across a stream since according to Tyler, the bridge had been washed out awhile back. Tyler and Harper had no problem jumping from stone to stone to get to the other side, but I knew that Zoe and Coker, the two babbits, would not be able to make it across with our packs. When no one was looking, I picked up Zoe first and tossed him to the other side, and before Coker could protest, I picked him up and threw him too. Just as he landed, Tyler turned around, looked at me still on the opposite side of the stream, and yelled, 'Hurry up, you slowpoke!' When I got to the other side, Zoe, Coker and I all laughed quietly amongst ourselves at our little stunt and continued up the path.

"I won't bore you with all the details," Titus told his sisters and parents, "but although the path was steep and rocky, we were up to the snow level in no time. Zoe ran ahead to Tyler and asked him if we could stop for a break. Tyler found an overlook that was warm and dry from the afternoon sun, and we stopped for a break. Harper laid out a tablecloth and proceeded to take out sandwiches, bottles of water, lots of fruit and cookies for dessert.

"The view from the overlook was spectacular. Tyler pointed to a small village where the babbits lived and then pointed to the island of Sanderling where the puppies live. Harper pointed south and said if you squinted real hard, you may be able to see Puffin Village.

"I asked Tyler how far it was to the top, and he said it was only about another two hours. I really wanted to get to the top before I woke up, so after we finished eating our fruit and sandwiches, we all decided to save our cookies for later and put them in the backpack. Zoe and Coker were smiling as we headed up the mountain because now their packs were lighter.

"The trail started to get narrow, and it was covered with snow. Harper told me that this is why we needed a guide because otherwise, we could get lost. As the trail wound around the mountain, we came upon a large cave. There was loud snoring coming from the cave, and I started getting a bit nervous.

"Tyler told us to wait here, and he would go in the cave to check it out. No sooner did he disappear in the darkness of the cave then we heard a loud roar and then a scream. Zoe and Coker were already running back down the path, and Harper and I looked at each other trying to decide what to do. Before we could move, a large white furry animal, which looked like a cross between a polar bear and a gorilla, came out carrying Tyler in his arms."

"What did you do?" asked Constance, holding her Remy stuffed animal tight.

Titus continued, "I reached for my six-gun I had on my last visit, but forgot I didn't have it. Harper told me to try and distract the creature while he tried to get Tyler away. I raised my arms over my head to make myself look bigger and let out a loud roar of my own. This made the creature laugh and drop Tyler in the snow. Harper grabbed Tyler and said, 'Let's run for it!' Tyler started laughing along with the creature. As it turns out, the creature was a good friend of Tyler's, and they do this joke every time Tyler guides real-worlders up the mountain.

"Tyler told me the bear's name was Sebastian, and he was a Yeti from Nepal. Sebastian was the guardian of Mount Pleasant, and his job was to make sure people didn't litter or cause any damage to the mountain.

"Tyler told Sebastian that he had another tour tomorrow at the same time, so he needed to be ready to roar when he came in the cave. He also said that they needed to leave now if they wanted to make it to the top of the mountain by sunset. When Tyler got back on the trail, he whistled real loud, and Zoe and Coker came running. As it turns out, they were in on the joke too.

"After another hour of hiking, they made it to the top just in time to watch the sunset. The view was breathtaking. The sun set in a large orange ball right into the ocean, while a flock of some kind of bird flew through the middle of the sun.

"From up north, Harper could see the smoke from a train, which was a reddish color from the sunset. Tyler told Harper that was the last train for the day so they needed to get down fast if they wanted to catch it for the trip back to Puffin Village. As it turns out, just on the other side of the mountain peak was the nest of Hunter, the large eagle that lived on top of Mount Pleasant. Tyler asked Hunter if he could fly Harper and Titus down to the station, and Hunter agreed as long as Tyler waited at the nest to keep an eye on the baby eagles.

"Next thing we knew, Harper and I were hanging on for our lives on the back of the eagle, as he slowly circled around to get us to the station without falling off. We got to the station with minutes to spare. We thanked Hunter and boarded the train as Hunter flew back up to the top of the mountain."

"That was a great adventure, Evie, and I will have to go there in a future dream," Constance said.

"Yes," said Titus, "flying on the back of the eagle was the best thing I have done so far in Dreamland. Hunter showed me how to do a special whistle, so if I ever need him, he will show up.

"Constance, where do you want to go for our dream tonight?" asked Titus.

"I don't know," said Constance.

"How about we meet at Harper and Remy's house and take the pirate ship to Sanderling Island and meet the puppies?" Titus asked.

"That sounds like fun," agreed Constance. "I will start thinking about what I will wear for the trip. See you at Harper and Remy's."

CHAPTER 11

The Pirate Ship

Titus and Constance woke up on the pirate ship in the captian's quarters. When they came out, Harper and Remy were busy putting supplies below deck. They had already loaded barrels of water, apples and flour, along with smoked ham, bacon and dried beef.

"Did you remember to bring dessert?" asked Titus.

"Sure enough," said Harper. "We loaded apple, pecan, cherry and blackberry pies, along with lots of snacks. "Where's Evie?" Harper asked.

"I don't think she is going to make this dream," Constance said. "Last I heard she was in her crib crying and mom and dad were with her. I hope she isn't coming down with something."

"Maybe she will join us later," Remy added.

"Harper," Titus called out, "how are we going to get the pirate ship from your backyard to the ocean?"

"It's your dream, Titus. Figure something out while Remy and I finish getting the ship ready to go."

"Titus, do you think my outfit looks good for the journey?" Constance asked. She was wearing a pair of cutoff blue jeans over stripped red and white leggings, black shoes with large silver buckles where the shoelaces should be, a matching black belt with a silver buckle and a long thin rubber dagger tucked in her belt. Constance also had on a red blouse tucked into her jeans and a matching blue denim vest. Around her neck she had a pucka shell necklace with a large shark tooth in the center. On her head, she had a red scarf tied tight like the pirates used to wear.

Titus whistled at Constance. "Wow, your outfit looks fantastic! Now I need to figure out how to get our ship to the ocean," Titus said.

Within minutes, the ship was utterly shaded from the sun. Titus looked up thinking that maybe the weather had changed and a storm was coming in. Instead, he saw Sebastian the giant eagle and a friend circling over the ship.

"You whistled?" asked Sebastian.

"Yes," said Titus, a little embarrassed that he whistled at Constance's outfit and not to call Sebastian. Titus, thinking quickly, figured out that Sebastian may be the solution to get the ship to the ocean, so he asked Sebastian if he and his friend could fly the ship to the ocean.

"That's not a friend. That's my wife, Mandy," Sebastian shouted down.

"Who is watching the baby eagles?" Titus asked.

"Tyler, of course. He was taking another group up Mount Pleasant when you whistled so I asked if he could stay and watch the eaglets. Let me know when you are ready to go!" Sebastian called out.

Titus gave two thumbs up to signal that he was ready. Sebastian used his giant claws to grab the foremast, while Mandy grabbed on the mast and slowly lifted the ship up in the air.

Flying on a ship over Puffin Village reminded Constance of the story of Peter Pan, which her dad read to them a while back. It was when Peter Pan returned Wendy, John, Michael and the lost boys to London on a pirate ship. "Hey Titus, doesn't this remind you of Peter Pan?" shouted Constance.

"It sure does," said Titus, "but in our dream, there won't be any kid-eating alligators," added Titus.

The ship barely cleared the church steeple, knocking the weather vane on top enough to set it spinning and making the large church bell ring. Within minutes, Sebastian and Mandy set the ship down in the center of Puffin Harbor. The water was calm, and there were large, white, puffy clouds in the sky. Harper dropped anchor to keep the ship from drifting into the rocks. Titus asked Harper why he dropped the anchor if they were about ready to sail to Sanderling Island.

Harper said, "Because we still have to set the sails and finish preparing the ship for our voyage."

Harper asked Titus and Constance how much they knew about sailing. Titus and Constance said, "Not much." Harper and Remy spent an hour going over the basics of sailing a ship with the two kids. They assigned Constance to take the wheel which steers the ship, while everyone else worked the sails to get the ship ready to go.

As they were about ready to go, Evie arrived on deck still wearing her pajamas. "Sorry for not changing, but I just fell asleep and I didn't want to miss the ship," said Evie.

"Okay," said Harper, "you can get changed later. For now, climb up to the crow's nest and keep an eye out for rocks or other ships."

Evie nodded her head and started climbing up to the crow's nest, which was on the main mast around 60 feet above the deck. From there, she could see over 15 miles away in every direction. Once she was settled in, she opened up her toy spyglass telescope she received for her birthday and scanned the horizon for rocks and ships.

With the rigging ready to go, Harper yelled out to hoist the anchor. It took all the strength of Harper, Remy and Titus combined to get the anchor back in the ship.

"That was a lot of work for a dream," Titus said. "I think I am going to dream up an automatic anchor hoister before my next sailing trip."

With the sun to their backs, they made their way out of the harbor and into Shearwater Ocean. Constance was busy keeping the ship heading due west, while Titus and Harper were in the captain's quarters, charting the course to Sanderling Island. Remy was already preparing breakfast for everyone in the ship's galley. Remy brought Harper and Titus plates of smoked bacon and scrambled eggs, as well as a loaf of freshly baked bread and a pitcher of milk. Next, she brought Constance and Evie breakfast sandwiches with bacon and eggs between two slices of bread, knowing they couldn't do their jobs while eating off plates.

With the course set, Titus relieved Constance at the wheel, and Constance climbed up to the crow's nest to give Evie a break. Using Evie's toy spyglass, Constance spotted a small ship heading their direction.

"Ship off our bow (bow is the front of the ship) about 2 miles," Constance yelled down. Harper, Remy and Titus all pulled out spyglasses to look at the ship.

"It looks like a small cargo ship heading to Puffin Village to get supplies for Sanderling Island," said Harper.

"Yes, but is has cannons and is flying a flag I don't recognize," said Remy.

"Titus to be safe, go arm the cannon. Remy, go below and get the bull horn. Evie, take control of the wheel and steer to the starboard (right side) of the ship. We want to keep the wind with us should we have to get out of here quickly," Harper added.

As the two ships got closer, Harper yelled, "Ahoy there, what is the name of your ship and where are you heading?"

A large Great Dane puppy wearing a captain's hat and a blue scarf yelled back, "This is the ship Sanderling Cloud, and we are heading to Puffin Village for supplies." Then the Great Dane puppy yelled back, "What is the name of your ship, and why are you flying a pirate flag? We were about to open fire on you when one of the crew spotted the human girl in the crow's nest."

Harper turned to Titus and asked, "What is the name of our ship?"

"Let's call it the USS Puffin, and let's take down the pirate flag before we get blown out of the water by mistake," suggested Titus.

Harper shouted back to the dogs, "Our ship is called the USS Puffin, and we are on a peaceful mission to explore Dreamland. Right now, we are sailing to Sanderling Island."

They lowered the pirate flag and replaced it with a new white and blue striped flag. The new flag had a Puffin bird in the center and it was the flag of Puffin Village. Once the puppy crew saw the new flag, they knew they were no longer in danger and moved away from the cannons.

The captain of Sanderling Cloud asked the crew of the USS Puffin if they would like to come aboard and join them for a snack. Titus couldn't picture everyone sitting on the floor eating dog food from a bowl, so he asked Remy to make some sandwiches to take with them just in case. As soon as the two ships were side by side and tied together, everyone used ropes to swing over like the pirates did in the stories, and they were on the deck of the Sanderling Cloud in no time. There must have been twenty puppies of different sizes, colors and breeds waiting on the deck to greet them.

"Hi, my name is Dane, and I am the captain of this ship. My first officer is Pete, and this is Bill, our navigator."

Pete was a white miniature schnauzer, about a third of the size of Dane. Bill was a hound dog with big droopy eyes and ears.

Harper introduced Remy and said they both lived in Puffin Village. Next, he introduced the Drapkin children and said they were real-worlders on a dream adventure. Dane said he also had a real-worlder, but he was from England and was probably awake and in school now. Dane, Pete and Bill led the group to the ship's mess hall (dining room) and everyone sat on large wooden benches around a table made out of weathered oak. To Titus's surprise and delight, the table had all kinds of cooked meats, baked bread, veggies and desserts. Although Titus, Constance and Evie just had breakfast, all they had to do was to dream they were hungry again. They did so and then filled their plates with their favorite foods.

"I have to admit," Titus said, with his mouth filled with mashed potatoes, "I thought we were going to have to eat dog food from bowls." Dane, Pete and Bill all howled with laughter, and Bill accidentally snorted out a pea from his nose, he as howling so hard.

"In Dreamland, we are actually as much like humans as we are like dogs," Dane said when he stopped howling.

After everyone was full and the table was cleared, Dane went over to the captian's quarters and brought back a map.

Pointing at a spot on the map, which was about twenty miles from Puffin Harbor, Dane said, "We are here, and this is where we are heading."

"That's Puffin Wharf," Remy said.

"Yes, we are supposed to be picking up supplies from Mr. Nordmo's General Store," Dane said.

"I believe all your supplies are already on the wharf because when we flew over the town, I saw one of Mr. Nordmo's helpers riding a large buckboard wagon full of supplies towards the direction of the wharf," Remy said.

"I'm sorry, did you say you flew over the town?" asked Bill, the hound dog.

"Yes," said Titus. "In my dream, I had two large eagles pick up the ship from town and bring it to the harbor."

"I forgot, anything is possible in Dreamland for real-worlders," Dane said. "Okay, now that you know where we are going, what are you going to do at Sanderling Island?" Dane asked.

"Since we have never been to Sanderling Island, what do you recommend?" Constance asked.

Dane pointed at the map. "You are here and over here is Sanderling Island. It is going to take you a full dream to get there." Dane turned the map over and on the backside was a large map of Sanderling Island. "As you can see, Sanderling is pretty large and each breed of dogs has their own village. However, right here," said Dane pointing to a spot on the map, "is the waterfront town of Port Kaynine. The waterfront is a bit rough, but once you get closer to the town center, there are a lot of attractions like restaurants and museums."

Dane continued talking and said, "I suggest for your next dream, you begin with your ship anchored in the harbor and take a dingy (small boat) to this wharf in the harbor. Make your way to Mrs. Harriet's Boarding House. She makes the best breakfast in Port Kaynine, and if you want to stay for more than one dream, this will be a good place to use as your base," Dane explained. "Tell Mrs. Harriet that you are friends of mine, and she will give you the puppy discount on food and lodging. Also, ask her for the map of the town. It will have all the places you will want to see clearly marked. This way, you can get the most out of your next dream."

With that, Dane rose and said it was time to head to Puffin Village since he had a schedule to keep. He wished them all a safe and fun voyage. Everyone went on deck, said their goodbyes and used the ropes to swing back to the USS Puffin. Both ships detached the ropes, and Harper ordered his crew to hoist all their sails to speed up their trip to Sanderling Island.

Evie, back up in the crow's nest, was the first to spot Sanderling Island. They sailed west to where Port Kaynine was. Although it was still far away, she could barely make out Port Kaynine since it was the largest of all the towns, and it spanned the entire beach of the harbor.

"Land Ho," Evie yelled down. "Keep heading west and we should be in the harbor in no time."

Everyone ran to the bow to see the town. Suddenly, Titus and Evie disappeared.

"Looks like Evie and Titus woke up," said Constance. "But I am still dreaming, so let's get in the dingy and head into town before I wake up!" As they started lowering the dingy, Constance disappeared too, leaving Harper and Remy on board the ship by themselves.

"I guess it is time for us to go back to the real world too and pretend like we are just stuffed animals until they wake up again," said Remy.

"Yep!" replied Harper. "Let's go."

CHAPTER 12

Port Kaynine

That night at dinner, Constance read her dream journal to her parents.

"I never did make it to Sanderling Island," Jack said. "I think it will be a great adventure exploring the island for your next dream."

"I am a little concerned about making our way through the waterfront to get into town," Constance admitted.

"Yes, waterfronts at port towns can be a bit rough," Jack said. "Can't you just start your dream in the center of town?" Jack asked.

Titus said, "Constance, Evie, remember how we had the squirrel clan scared because they thought we were gun-slingers? Well, why don't we enter the town as mean pirates and bring a change of clothes so when we get to Mrs. Harriet's Boarding House, we can change back into our street clothes?"

"That sounds like a great way to start a new dream adventure," said Constance, and Evie nodded her head in agreement.

So, after Jack read another chapter, all the kids went to bed. Before they fell asleep, they each dreamed about the pirate outfits they were going to wear for that night's dream. Titus dreamed of wearing black boots that came almost up to his knees, blue pants, a white shirt with ruffles on the front and a black sash around his waist and a blue vest with gold buttons. On his head, he had a tricorn hat with a skull and crossbones on the front. He also had a pirate buccaneer sword that he could put in his sash when he wasn't using it.

Constance dreamed about wearing brown knee-high boots, black pants, a long red jacket that went down to her knees with gold braids in front to keep the jacket closed instead of buttons. On her head she had the same style hat as Titus, but it was red with gold braided trim. To make herself look tough, she wore an eye patch and had a small dagger in her red sash.

Evie dreamed about wearing a black and white striped dress, with a black vest, a white ruffled shirt and a red bandana on her head. She even added a small black mustache that she drew on using her mother's eyebrow pencil.

When all three of the children arrived back on the ship, Harper and Remy were waiting for them dressed in pirate outfits too. The first thing Titus did was change the flag back to the pirate flag. They lowered the dingy and all climbed in. Titus and Constance both rowed while Evie was in the front directing them to the wharf.

The sun was just rising as they tied the boat to the wharf. Titus thought it would be safer to travel through the waterfront early in the morning when everyone was still sleeping. What he didn't realize was that Port Kaynine was the biggest port on Sanderling Island so ships were already loading or unloading goods and supplies.

As they walked down the wharf, no one took notice of the group since everyone was busy working. At the end of the wharf there were hundreds of puppies and dogs from Sanderling Island, as well as other animals from all parts of Dreamland. Titus saw mice, squirrels, bears, kumons, badgers, babbits and numerous other animals he had never seen before. Everyone was either rushing around to go somewhere, selling something or buying supplies.

"Do all these animals live in Dreamland?" Titus asked Harper.

"Yes," said Harper. "As you know, Dreamland is very large and since this is a port town, it attracts inhabitants from all parts. I have yet to travel to many parts of Dreamland, so there are animals here I have never seen before."

As they were making their way past the stalls filled with pigs, sheep, goats and turkeys and past the stalls selling vegetables, fish and oysters, Constance noticed two suspicious dogs following them. One dog was a mean-looking short, fat brown bulldog with a scar on his right cheek and he wore a worn leather vest, a belt with a large sword and a pirate hat. The other dog was a small dark gray pug with large bulging black eyes and a nose that looked like it had been punched more than a few times. It was hard to tell if the pug was watching them since his eyes went in two different directions.

"Titus, don't look now but I think we are being followed by two mean-looking dogs," Constance whispered.

Harper heard what Constance said and suggested they all go into the boat supply store they were just about to pass to see if the two dogs stopped or kept on walking. As they entered the store, the shopkeeper took one look at the group and told them that pirates were not welcome in his store. Harper tried to explain that they really weren't pirates but the small thin toy poodle store owner, clearly upset, started jumping up and down and running around in circles, yelping that he wanted them to leave immediately. As they turned around to leave, the pug and bulldog walked into the store and were face-to-face with the group.

"Why are you following us?" Titus confronted them in his loud, deep outside voice.

The pug had a "who me?" expression on his face and his eyes were going in all different directions. The bulldog, on the other hand, had a menacing snarl and asked, "Are you the real-worlders here for the treasure map?"

"What's it to you?" Titus replied, trying to figure out what he was referring to.

"Out of my store all you or I will call the police!" The toy poodle yapped with an annoyingly loud and high-pitched voice.

"Let's go down the street to the Green Parrot Saloon where we can talk," said the bulldog.

Since it was still very early in the morning, the Green Parrot Saloon was almost empty. At the bar, there was a three-legged terrier with an eye patch drinking something from a dark brown bottle along with a stray mutt that looked like it never took a bath. Both dogs seemed to be arguing over a dog bone on the bar. Besides these two, and the large French poodle waitress behind the bar, the rest of the place was empty.

The group found a large, round wooden table in the back of the dimly lit bar and sat down. Constance had her hand on her dagger under the table just in case this was some kind of funny business. Titus made sure he sat facing the door to watch if anyone suspicious came in. Evie kept her eye on the back door in case they had to make a quick exit.

The bulldog started talking first. "My name is Duke and this is my partner, Max. We were told to stay at the wharf until a group of real-world pirates showed up asking about a treasure map," Duke said.

"Okay, you figured us out. So, where is the treasure map?" Titus said trying to sound convincing.

"How do we know you are the right group of pirates?" Max asked suspiciously. His voice was very commanding for such a little dog.

"Whoever told you to look for us must have told you what to ask us to prove who we are," Constance said quickly.

"Yes," said Duke, "I am supposed to ask you two riddles that only the *real* pirates would know, and if you answer it correctly, I can tell you where to find the map."

"What is the first riddle?" Titus asked.

Max looked around to see if anyone was listening, then he leaned forward and asked, "What would a pirate say if he wanted a piece of wood placed in a barrel of ice-water?"

Everyone looked stumped. Titus glanced around at Constance and Evie but did not say anything. Max leaned over to Duke and said, "I don't think these are the right pirates. What do we do with them if they don't know the answer?"

After a long moment of silence, Duke moved his chair back and started to stand up and Max was reaching for something under the table when Evie shouted, "Shiver me timbers."

Titus was about to tell Evie to be quiet, when Duke said, "You are correct." Duke and Max sat back down. Constance was about ready to ask Evie how she knew the answer but decided it would be best to wait until later. Harper and Remy looked at each other, impressed that Evie knew the answer.

"So now that we answered the first riddle correctly, what is the second riddle?" Constance asked.

Max figured that the correct answer on the first riddle may have been lucky, but unless they were the real pirates, they wouldn't know the answer to the next riddle.

"What was the name of the young captain of the pirate ship Adventure Galley?"

Titus read lots of books on pirates and knew the names of most of the famous pirates, but he never bothered to memorize the name of their ships. Thinking to himself, he could remember Black Beard, Anne Bonny, Black Bart and Captain Morgan, but he couldn't remember the name of their ships.

Again Duke and Max started to stand up after it appeared that they didn't know the answer when Evie yelled out, "Captain Kid."

Titus looked at Evie in amazement and then added, "Yes, Captain William Kidd," hoping that Evie guessed correctly.

"That's right," said Duke.

Constance whispered into Evie's ear, "How did you know the name of the captain?"

Evie whispered back, "I didn't, I just guessed from the clues that he was a captain and he was young, and kids are young so that is why I guessed it was Captain Kid."

"That's a different type of kid, one is spelled with one d and the other with two," Constance told Evie.

"Well, they sound the same to me," Evie replied. Constance rolled her eyes but was happy Evie guessed right.

Duke and Max looked at each other and Duke said, "Max, it looks like we found the right group." Max nodded in agreement.

Duke went on to say, "Before Captian Kidd was captured, he spent his last night at Mrs. Harriet's Boarding House, up the hill at the end of Main Street. He hid a map to his treasure under the floorboards of the room he stayed in. Unfortunately, no one has ever found the map since he never told anyone which room he stayed in. Shortly after Captain Kidd checked out, he was captured and taken back for trial.

"If you are looking for clues as to which room he was in, you should try and question his parrot, which flew back to the boarding house when Captain Kidd was captured." At that point, Duke and Max stood up, turned around and left the bar.

"It looks like your dream has taken on a new twist. Harper and I have never been on a treasure hunt before, but it sounds like fun," Remy said to the group.

Constance, being better at organizing things than Titus, took charge and suggested that since they were going to go to Mrs. Harriet's Boarding House anyway, they should first go there for lunch, and, before checking in, try to question the parrot to find out which room they should ask for. The group agreed and started to head out of the bar. As they were about to leave, the two dogs that were arguing at the bar turned and the three-legged terrier put his crutch out to stop them.

The terrier with the crutch and eye patch said, "Did I hear correctly that you are hunting for a treasure map?"

Harper started to laugh and said, "I wish. I think you misunderstood what you heard. We were discussing going hunting for wild hamsters to take back home to sell as pets in Puffin Village. Since there is a size limit, we were going to set measure traps, to make sure the hamsters we catch meet the correct size. I can understand how you can confuse measure traps with treasure maps."

The terrier stared at Harper for a long time then removed his crutch from blocking their path and went back to arguing with mutt at the bar.

When they all got outside, Titus said, "That was quick thinking, Harper. Just in case they didn't believe you, let's keep an eye out to make sure they don't follow us."

As they made their way to Mrs. Harriet's Boarding House, they passed through the waterfront area and entered the fancy part of town. Everyone was dressed nicely and as they passed, many people were staring at them dressed in their pirate outfits.

Remy suggested they stop in a clothing store they were passing and use the changing room to get changed into their regular clothes, which Remy had been carrying in a backpack.

"This way, we will blend in with the townspeople and we will less likely be recognized if we are being followed," Remy added.

Fortunately, the store clerk was busy measuring a rather overweight large black female poodle with curly fur for a new dress, so he didn't notice the group enter the store. Soon, they were all changed into their street clothes and put the pirate outfits into the backpack.

After walking uphill for a while, they saw the boarding house at the end of the street. As they started to cross the street, Harper saw a large stagecoach coming right at them and yelled out to tell everyone to stop. The coach barely missed them, but its wheel went through a large puddle and threw muddy water on the group. This woke Titus, Constance and Evie up all at the same time.

Titus yelled in his bedroom. "No. Not again! Just when the dream was getting good."

Constance, used to this by now, got up and started writing in her dream journal so they could pick up at Mrs. Harriet's Boarding House. Evie started playing with her toes and cried out for her mother.

CHAPTER 13

Mrs. Harriet's Boarding House

At dinner that evening, Titus and Constance told their parents all about Port Kaynine, the waterfront, Duke and Max and how Evie solved the two riddles so they could get the treasure map. Tonight they planned on going back to Dreamland and start the dream outside Mrs. Harriet's Boarding House.

Jack and Mrs. Dapkin were both impressed with how the kids now went to bed without a struggle, how they slept through the night and how well they remembered what they dreamed. After dinner, chores, baths and bedtime stories were done, the kids were ready for sleep with no complaints.

When they arrived outside Mrs. Harriet's Boarding House, Harper and Remy were waiting for them. It was pitch black out so Titus thought it must be late in Dreamland.

"Guys, while we were here waiting for you to return, we saw a few rough-looking dogs entering the boarding house. One of them was the three-legged terrier from the Green Parrot Saloon," Harper told them.

"I don't think anyone will recognize you since you aren't wearing your pirate outfits, but be careful and keep your voices down just in case," Remy added.

The entrance to the lobby of the boarding house was through the pub and grill. The pub and grill was very dark, only lit by a few candles and a large fireplace in the corner. It took the group a minute for their eyes to adjust to the dark, but everyone in the pub was involved in their own conversations and took no notice of the group.

Remy found an empty table against the wall in a dark corner and the group sat down. The table was old and worn with initials and dates carved in the top and long benches on either side. A young puppy dressed in white pants, a white shirt, a blue sash and a blue bandana around his neck came over to the table with menus.

"Hi, my name is Riley and I will be your server. We are busy tonight, so I will give you a minute to look over the menu." Just as he said that the table across the room with all the mean-looking dogs and the terrier yelled at to Riley to get his tail over there and bring them more to drink.

Riley looked mad, then he took a deep breath and said, "Sorry about that group. As I said, we are busy so I will be right back."

While everyone was looking at the menu, Constance spotted Captain Kidd's parrot sitting on a tall wooden perch right near the mean dog group. Every now and then the parrot would screech out, "Pieces of eight, pieces of eight." No one paid any attention to it.

When Riley came back, he took everyone's order and then said, "We don't get many real-worlders here and the ones who do come are usually looking for Captian Kidd's treasure map."

Titus, Constance and Evie all tried to look surprised.

"If that is why you are here, you can forget it because I have searched this whole place and I didn't find it."

Before he could finish, the terrier yelled, "Hey boy, we need more drinks and bring some of your best steaks over because we are all hungry."

Riley took off to the kitchen to place the order. This gave the group time to discuss what Riley had said and how they should try to talk with the parrot.

"This is good," said Harper.

"How can this be good?" Titus questioned. "We have a bunch of mean dogs between the parrot and us, and Riley has already searched the whole place."

"It's good because the map hasn't been found yet," Harper responded.

Riley came out with bread, butter and water for everyone.

"Riley do you have crackers in the kitchen?" Constance asked.

110

"Sure, we are a pub and grill," Riley answered.

"Can you bring a few over next time you come by?" Constance asked.

"No problem," Riley responded.

"Hey boy! Where are our steaks?" the terrier yelled.

"They are still cooking," Riley responded politely.

"Did I ask you to cook them?" the terrier yelled back. "Did anyone in this room hear me ask the boy to cook the steaks?"

Silence followed.

"Didn't think so. Get those steaks off the grill and bring them to us NOW!" the terrier yelled.

Riley turned red with embarrassment and anger and went stomping off to the kitchen to get the steaks and crackers. First, he brought the crackers to Constance. Next, he brought the steaks to the terrier and dropped them all on the top of the terrier's head.

The terrier got angry and yelled, "Why did you do that?"

Riley shouted loudly, "Did anyone in the room hear the terrier tell me not to put the steaks on his head?"

Silence followed.

"I didn't think so." And with that Riley raced out the door with the mean group of dogs and the terrier chasing after him.

This was the opportunity Constance was looking for. She took the crackers and went over to the parrot. "Polly want a cracker?" Constance asked.

The parrot squawked and then screeched, "Pieces of eight, pieces of eight," and took the cracker.

Constance looked around to make sure the mean dogs hadn't returned and then whispered into the parrot's ear, "Where is Captian Kidd's treasure map?"

The parrot responded, "Pieces of eight, pieces in eight." Constance gave the parrot the last cracker and went back to the group.

Just as she sat down, the mean dog group came back in huffing and puffing, apparently unable to catch young Riley.

"So, which room is the treasure map in?" Titus asked.

"Room eight," Constance responded. "The parrot said pieces of 8 are in room eight."

"Say what? I didn't hear him say that," Titus responded.

"Well, what he said was pieces of 8, pieces in 8," Constance clarified.

"That is kind of a stretch, but it is all we have to work with for now," Titus said.

With Riley missing, Gunther, the old hound dog who was the cook, brought all the food to the table and everyone chowed down.

While the group was eating, Harper and Remy went to the front desk to reserve the room. After waiting a few minutes for a clerk, they hit the bell on the counter to get some help. From under the desk, a small old English toy spaniel hopped onto the counter and said, "Good evening, I am Mrs. Harriet the third. How can I help you?"

"I would like a room for tonight for my sister and me," Harper requested.

"Okay, sign here."

On the counter, there was an old book with pages of signatures. "That will be five dollars," Mrs. Harriet said and then gave them the key for room four.

"Is it possible to have room eight for tonight?" Harper asked.

"Impossible," the spaniel said. "The last person who stayed in that room really messed it up searching for a treasure map, and we have not had time to clean it."

Remy pretended to cry and Harper said, "Now look what you've done. You've made my sister cry. Every time we come here, we stay in room eight, and now you tell us we can't."

"Suit yourself," Mrs. Harriet said in an annoyed voice. "Here is the key for room eight, but don't come back and complain about the room."

Remy smiled and gave the spaniel a big hug, and they both went back to the table.

"It wasn't easy, but we got room eight. Apparently, the last person who stayed tore the room up looking for the map," Remy said.

"I hope they didn't find it," Evie whispered.

"To not raise any suspension, I think we should go up in pairs, a few minutes apart. Harper and I will go first, followed by Constance and Evie, and when it is clear no one is following us, Titus will come up last," Remy told them.

Harper and Remy left money to cover the dinner and headed up the stairs. Room eight was up a dark and windy set of wooden stairs that led to the second floor. There was only one candle mounted on the wall of the staircase and one in the hall on the second floor. When they checked in, the clerk gave them each a candle to use in the room. When they got to the second floor, they used the candle mounted on the wall to light their candles. This brightened up the hall and made it easier to find room eight.

After putting the key in the lock and opening the door, Harper and Remy found the room was a total mess. The bed had been turned upside down, the paintings had been removed and the backs opened, some of the wallpaper was peeled off and all the drawers in the dresser were removed and laying in a pile. Constance and Evie arrived next, followed shortly by Titus.

Given that the room was small and had furniture spread all over the place, Titus could barely get into the room and close the door.

"Constance, you pick up all the drawers and put them back in the dresser. Evie, you collect all the paintings and lean them against the wall. Remy, you can turn the table and chair over while Titus and I put the bed against the wall and roll up the carpet," Harper directed.

Once the room was in order and the carpet had been rolled up, Constance noticed how many planks there were on the floor. "We could be here all night lifting up planks and looking for the map," Constance said.

"Haven't you heard about the pirates using an X to mark the spot?" Titus asked Constance.

"Yes, but I thought that was only for finding hidden treasure," Constance responded.

"Well, let's hope they also use it to find the treasure maps," Titus said.

Titus got down on the floor. Using one of the candles, he started checking out each plank. In a matter of minutes, he found a plank that had a small X scratched in the corner.

"Look here," Titus said. "I think this may be the spot."

Constance got down, and using her dagger, she slowly started prying the plank up. Every time she lifted the plank, it made a loud cracking sound. After prying it up about 3 inches, Titus used the candlelight

115

to see if anything was under the plank. Sure enough, there was an old piece of leather wrapped around something with a string around it.

Titus tried to reach in, but his hand was too large. As he was about to ask Constance to pry it up higher, Evie reached in and grabbed the leather roll. Constance slowly let down the plank, while Titus and Remy put the carpet back into position and then placed the bed back on top of the carpet.

Evie removed the string from the leather and unrolled it on the table. After everyone quit sneezing from the dust that had flown in their faces from opening the map, they could make out a detailed map of Sanderling Island. The map was drawn on parchment paper and clearly very old. Many of the landmarks on the map were so faded they could not be read.

Looking over the map, they found Port Kaynine, which was on the east coast of the island—about halfway between the south and the north parts of the island. On the very northwest part of the island was Bounty Bay and slightly inland from the bay was a large X. Next to the X were directions on how to locate the treasure.

"Eureka!" Evie shouted. Excitement filled the room. Since Harper and Remy had never been to Sanderling Island, they did not recognize any of the trails, towns or other landmarks on the map.

"I have an idea," said Titus. "If we all leave for the ship, the mean dogs will probably figure out we have the map and follow us. How about Harper, Remy and Evie head to the ship and if the mean dogs follow, you sail around until you lose them. Then, head to Bounty Bay. While you're doing that, Constance and I will use the bedsheets to climb out of the window and head up this trail." Titus pointed to a trail on the map. "This will take us over land to the treasure. If we get there first, we will start digging up the treasure and meet you on the beach."

Harper, Remy and Evie thought it was a good plan. Harper used a small piece of paper to copy the map just in case they got there first.

The sun was just rising as Harper, Remy and Evie made their way down the stairs. Every step they took made the stairs creak loudly. When they got to the lobby, they looked into the pub and noticed the mean dogs were all sleeping at the table, right where they were the night before.

Quietly, the group made their way past the dogs and to the front door. As the door opened, it made a squeaking sound that woke up the parrot. It squawked, "Pieces of 8, pieces of 8."

The terrier opened his eyes to see the group go out the front door. While the terrier was looking for his crutch and waking the other dogs, Harper, Remy and Evie were able to flag down a passing carriage. They asked if they could get a lift to the wharf at Port Kaynine. The driver told them that was where he was heading and as they pulled away, Evie saw all the mean dogs come out of the pub and look around for them.

The carriage was halfway down Main Street before the dogs figured out what happened. All the dogs, except for the terrier who was using a crutch, started running after the carriage.

In the meantime, Titus and Constance had finished tying sheets together and had climbed out the window with the map. The sun was just beginning to rise, but it was still dark outside when they found the trail marked on the map.

After walking for over an hour, they stopped to rest near a stream. As they were making their way from the path down to the stream, Titus heard the sound of footsteps and twigs breaking from the path they had just walked. Thinking it was the mean dogs, Titus told Constance to hide. Titus got behind a tree and crouched with a large stick hovering over his head in case he needed to use it.

From behind Titus came a voice.

"What are we hiding from?" asked Riley.

"I heard someone following us," Titus began to answer. In mid-sentence, it dawned on him that it was Riley, their waiter from Mrs. Harriet's Boarding House who was following them.

"What are you doing following us?" asked Titus.

"Since I lost my temper and my job at Mrs. Harriet's Boarding House, I had nowhere to go. Then I started thinking, maybe your group was there for the map, and maybe you had a clue to where it was hidden. When I noticed candles in room eight and heard furniture moving around, I assumed you were looking for the map. When I saw you and Constance go out the window, I knew you had found it," Riley said.

"So what if we did find the map. We found it and you didn't. Why should we let you in on the treasure?" Constance asked.

"First off, I have a bag with supplies and water. Next, I know Sanderling Island very well, and I know which towns we can visit and which ones we should avoid. And last, if the treasure is there, from what I understand, there will be more than enough for everyone to share," Riley answered.

After Constance and Titus spoke, Titus agreed to allow Riley to join them on the treasure hunt. After all, it was a dream and Constance and Titus were taught to share with others, so why not give Riley a share of the treasure if he helped them find it?

The carriage dropped the group off at the end of the wharf at the place where the driver had to go to pick up a group of vacationing squirrels from Willets. Harper, Remy and Evie managed to get into the dingy, untie it and cast off before the mean dogs could reach them. As they were rowing out to their ship, Remy could see the terrier, which just caught up with the group, talking to captains. It appeared that he was trying to hire a ship to follow them.

Harper, Remy and Evie made it to the ship and quickly used Titus's steam-powered anchor hoister invention to pull the anchor up. Right after they set sail, Evie spotted a small but fast schooner heading their way. A schooner is a smaller two-mast ship designed more for speed than for carrying a lot of cargo. Harper plotted a course that took them in the direction of Puffin Village to see if the schooner was following them. While this was happening, Titus had opened the map so Riley could figure out the best route to the treasure.

"I suggest we stay on this path until we reach Flea Town. The town is an old mining camp, and the dogs and puppies are very friendly there. We can get lunch and any additional supplies we will need there," Riley said.

"I thought dogs hated fleas?" Titus said.

Riley laughed and said, "We do hate fleas, but it is called Flea Town because it is the home to the most famous flea circus in all of Dreamland. When we get there, we have to go and visit the flea circus and the Flea Museum.

"As real-worlders, you will probably have to wake up around that time, and this will be a good place for me to wait until you return," Riley added.

"How do we know you won't go on and look for the treasure yourself?" Constance asked Riley.

"Do I look like the type of puppy who would double-cross my new friends?" Riley asked.

"No, I guess not," Constance answered.

The trail looked big on the map, but in reality, it wasn't much more than a mountain goat path. Most of the trail was winding uphill around a mountain peak. As they got higher, they could almost see the whole island. When they stopped to rest, Riley pointed out different parts of Sanderling Island.

"To my east, is Port Kaynine. You can see the wharf and almost make out Mrs. Harriet's Boarding House on the hill. To the south, is the port town of Coonhound. To the southeast is Mongrel Village and to the west is Wolf Dog Harbor. Way up northeast is Bounty Bay where the treasure is buried, and that little speck down there is Flea Town, where we are heading," Riley pointed out to Titus and Constance.

Back on the ship, Evie made her way up to the crow's nest. She could see that the schooner was still following them. She yelled down to Remy, who was at the wheel. Remy yelled to Harper, who was in the captain's cabin, looking over the map.

Harper came out and said that he had a plan. Speaking loudly so Evie could hear him, he told the group, "We should continue back to Puffin Village to draw the schooner away from the treasure, and while we are there, we can resupply the ship. When the coast is clear, we should head to Bounty Bay and pick up the others."

Everyone agreed with the plan, so they lowered the pirate flag, raised the Puffin Village flag and hoisted all the sails to get to Puffin Village quickly.

Shortly, Evie yelled, "Land ho!"

As the ship made its way into the harbor, they spotted a place on the wharf where they could tie up the ship. Although they made good time with full sails. Before Remy could finish tying up the ship, the terrier and the pit bull jumped onto the wharf and were waiting by the ship. Harper, Remy and Evie walked down the ramp and tried to ignore the two dogs on the wharf.

"Where are the others?" the terrier called out in a loud voice.

"What others?" Evie asked.

The pitbull ran up the ramp and quickly searched every part of the ship. When he came up to the top deck, he yelled down to the terrier that the ship was empty.

"Looks like we were tricked," said the terrier. "The others must still be on the island searching for the treasure."

"How will we find them now that they have such a long headstart?" asked the pit bull.

"Easy," said the Terrier. "We sail back to Port Kaynine, and when we get to Mrs. Harriet's Boarding House, we convince Gunther, the hound dog cook, to help us track the others. He used to be a tracker for the military, so he is really good at picking up scents."

With that, the two dogs hopped back on the schooner and started sailing back to Port Kaynine.

"That was close," said Harper. "Too bad we can't warn Titus and Constance."

"Since it is almost time to wake up, I can warn them when I see them in the morning," Evie said.

"I thought you were still too young to talk," Remy said.

"I have been working on it, and now I can say a few words," Evie replied.

"Okay. While you are gone, Harper and I will resupply the ship and be ready to sail when you return," Remy answered. "By the way, your dad will have a surprise for you this evening. I can't tell you what it is but—"

Before Remy could finish the sentence, Evie was gone and awake in her crib.

Riley, Titus and Constance just made it down to Fea Town when Constance heard the soft cry of Evie.

"Looks like we are about to wake up," said Constance.

"See the Flea Museum down the street on the right?" Riley asked. "I will meet you both there when you return."

Titus and Constance agreed and both woke up.

CHAPTER 14

Millie

Evie woke the whole family up crying. Mrs. Drapkin went into her room to see what was wrong. Evie said, "Hungry." Now that she could speak a few words, she could say why she was upset.

After breakfast and chores, the kids went out to play since it was Saturday and no one had school. While they were in the backyard alone, Evie said to Titus and Constance, "Mean dogs."

Confused, Titus asked, "What about the mean dogs? Were they following us?"

Evie nodded. Constance smiled and said, "Thanks for letting us know; we will keep an eye out for them when we return."

That night at dinner, Jack came in late with a package under his arm. He placed the package on the counter and sat down to eat with the family.

"What's in the package?" Titus asked.

"It's a surprise for Evie," Jack whispered to Titus. He changed the subject and asked about last night's adventure.

Constance told her dad about the boarding house, the mean dogs that were keeping an eye on them, the parrot giving them a clue to the treasure map, how they found the map under the floorboards and how Evie, Harper and Remy lead the mean dogs away with the ship while Titus and Constance went out the window to follow the trail to the treasure.

Titus told about Riley, the pup from Mrs. Harriet's Boarding House, and how Riley was helping them find the treasure. "Tonight we are meeting Riley at the Flea Museum in Flea Town, and I think Evie is going back to the ship with Harper and Remy."

Evie nodded.

That evening after everyone was in bed and read to, Jack went into Evie's room with the package he had brought from the toy store. As he opened it, Evie could see a large matchbox like the ones Harper and Remy slept in.

"A week ago, while you were off in Dreamland, I designed a new Dreamland animal of your own," Jack said. In the box was a cute little girly mouse. "Her name is Millie, and she is all yours," Jack added.

Evie was so excited to have her own Dreamland animal. Before leaving the room, Jack put out the candles in Evie's room. He left a little candle near her crib to be a nightlight.

Soon, everyone was asleep. Titus and Constance found themselves back in Dreamland sitting on a wooden bench in front of the Flea Museum, and Evie found herself on the ship standing next to Millie, her new Dreamland friend.

"I see you've met Millie," Remy said to Evie. "She was the surprise I was trying to tell you about. Millie is our cousin who lives on the other side of Puffin Village. She just turned five and is now old enough for her own real-worlder. We instantly thought of you!"

"I think Millie and I are going to be great friends," said Evie.

The ship was fully loaded, so Harper gave the order to set sail. Evie and Millie climbed up to the crow's nest to keep an eye out for other ships, while Remy sailed the ship and Harper looked at the map in the captain's quarters.

Millie told Evie about her family in Puffin Village. She has an older brother and an older sister, who tease her a lot, but it's always in a friendly way. Both her brother and sister already had real-worlder friends and got to go on all kinds of adventures. For the rest of the voyage, Evie and Millie got to know each other better while keeping a lookout in the crow's nest.

Titus was just about to go into the museum when the flea at the ticket counter told him a ticket cost five dollars.

"That seems like a lot because the museum is small," Titus said in a questioning tone.

The flea was offended and said, "Because this is the best flea museum in all of Dreamland, we charge a little more than the other museums."

Just as Titus was about to say something, Riley came out of the museum.

"That was great," Riley said to the flea. "I didn't want to leave."

Titus was confused about how a flea museum could be so fascinating to Riley since he was a puppy, but Titus wanted to get on with the adventure, so he didn't ask.

Flea Town looked a lot like Willets, only older and more run down. There were wooden buildings on either side of a dirt street, tumbleweeds blowing down Main Street and wooden planks for sidewalks covered with dust and mud.

Riley suggested they head over to Tater Tot's Café and have breakfast while they discussed the next part of the journey. Tater Tot's was a brightly lit little café with blue and white ruffled curtains. Inside were ten tables with matching blue and white checkered tablecloths. There were two fleas sitting at the counter having a discussion about the flea circus, and a small, old Boston terrier with a blue and white apron was serving them coffee.

The Boston terrier next came over to the group's table with menus and said, "Good morning. My name is Ms. Tater Tot. Welcome to my café. Today's blue plate special is bacon and eggs with homemade tater tots and freshly baked biscuits for $4.99."

Everyone ordered the blue plate special, and Ms. Tater Tot went into the kitchen to start making their meals.

When no one was around, Riley spread the map out on the table. "We are here, and we have two ways we can get to Bounty Bay. We can take this ridge trail," Riley said pointing to a trail on the map, "which will be a little tough and may have some snow, or we can descend this path to Wolf Dog Harbor and then follow the shoreline road. The second choice is easier, but it is also longer." Riley traced the trails on the map.

"There is one other thing to consider," Titus told Riley. "When we woke up in the real world, Evie warned us that the mean dogs may be back on our track."

"Those dogs couldn't track a wagon of steaks," Riley said. "To follow our trail, you would need a real tracker like Gunther, the bloodhound cook at Mrs. Harriet's Boarding House."

"The mean dogs are probably going to Mrs. Harriet's Boarding House since that is where we lost them. What if they offer Gunther part of the treasure? Do you think he would track us?" asked Constance.

"Most likely," said Riley. "Gunther always talked about how much he hated being a cook and how much he wanted to spend his days as a tracker. That kind of money would allow him to quit his job and become a tracker again."

"If Gunther is tracking us, that changes everything. I suggest we take the third choice. We buy a canoe and take the Hunter River, which flows all the way to Bounty Bay. If we are in the water, Gunther will not be able to track us," Riley added as he rolled up the map and gave it back to Titus.

"That seems the easiest and fastest route. How come you didn't suggest that before?" asked Constance.

"Because there are several rapids and waterfalls along the river, so it will be challenging and a bit dangerous," Riley said.

By now, the terrier and the mean dogs had made it back to Mrs. Harriets' Boarding House. A new little blonde toy poodle with a white apron, named Missy, came over to take their order. After they placed their order, the terrier asked the waitress to have Gunther come out when he was free. When the order was done, the toy poodle and Gunther came to deliver the food.

"Missy," said Gunther to the poodle. "I am taking a five-minute break. You should too before the lunch rush starts." With that, Missy went into the backroom to powder her fur and add more lipstick.

"What's up, guys?" asked Gunther.

The Terrier told Gunther about the real-worlders finding the treasure map and asked if he would help track them down. The terrier promised Gunther part of the treasure if he helped.

"I'll tell you what," said Gunther, "the pub and grill is closed between lunch and dinner so I should have just enough time to get you on the right path."

"If you don't go with us the entire way, you will only get a small share of the treasure. But, if you track the real-worlders all the way to the treasure, you will get a larger share," the terrier told Gunther.

"Sorry, I can't just quit my job and leave Mrs. Harriet without a cook," Gunther said. "As much as I would like to have a bigger share, it isn't right to walk out of a job without notice."

Gunther didn't trust the terrier anyway. Even if they found the treasure, Gunther figured the terrier and the mean dogs would do something so he wouldn't get a share.

When Gunther finished his break and went back to cooking, the terrier told the group that he had no intentions on sharing the treasure with Gunther anyway. If Gunther only got them on the right trail, the group could probably follow the trail, find the real-worlders and get the treasure without having to share it with Gunther.

Finally, after the lunch rush was over, Gunther walked outside below the window of room eight with the terrier and mean dogs following.

As Gunther sniffed around, he found the scent of Titus and Constance. He followed the trail up into the mountains and found the spot where the kids walked down to the water. Gunther picked up the scent of Riley at the same spot. Although Riley quit and left him working the shift by himself, he still liked Riley and didn't want the mean dogs after Riley so he didn't mention Riley to the pack.

The terrier could tell something was wrong by the way Gunther was acting. "You better tell us the right path, or we will come back and tear up the boarding house," the terrier threatened Gunther.

"Calm down," said Gunther. "It looks like the real-worlders took this path to Flea Town. Once you get there, you can ask some locals which way the real-worlders went."

Gunther went back to Mrs. Harriet's Boarding House while the pack of mean dogs headed up the mountain pass to get to Flea Town.

Evie, Millie, Harper and Remy had sailed the ship to the east coast of Sanderling Island. They chose to stop in Wolf Dog Harbor because if Titus and Constance chose to take the shoreline trail, they might be able to meet up at the harbor and sail together to Bounty Bay.

As Riley, Titus and Constance were leaving Tater Tot's Café, Titus spotted a large poster on the front of the post office announcing the flea circus.

"Look, they have a show just about to start! Do you think we have time to watch some of the circus?" asked Titus.

"I've seen it before and it is worth seeing," said Riley. "How about you and Constance go watch the show while I go and buy a shovel, pick and canoe. The circus tent is on the other end of town, near the river. I will pop in the hardware store and meet you by the river in an hour," Riley said.

Titus and Constance purchased tickets and snacks and found a front seat near the main ring. Constance couldn't wait to eat the cotton candy and popcorn. The tent was packed with dogs, puppies and fleas from all parts of the island.

The ringmaster had just announced the next act. Six huge Great Dane puppies entered the ring and arranged themselves in a circle. Fleas doing tricks jumped from one puppy to the next. When the act was over, the ringmaster pointed to a large cage to his left. Inside the cage were wild-looking kittens. The circus fleas used small chairs and ropes to get the kittens to perform stunts. One kitten caught a rope and pulled it from the hands of one of the flea trainers. Just when a group of kitten herders were about to enter the cage to catch the bad kitten, the kitten dropped the rope and went back to strike a pose.

Titus looked up and saw five fleas doing death-defying acts on a trapeze without a net. One of the fleas did a triple somersault while flying between two swings. As this act was going on, a small carriage, pulled by a chihuahua puppy, stopped in the middle of the ring. Within seconds, over 100 fleas dressed like clowns got out of the carriage and started to hop on each other's shoulders. Soon, all 100 fleas were stacked up high enough to reach the trapeze. Each of the trapeze artists crawled down the flea ladder. Just as the last trapeze artist was down, the group lost its balance and clown fleas went everywhere. Some landed on the Great Danes, some on top of the kitten cage and two landed in the tub of popcorn on Constance's lap. She let out a laugh.

The ringmaster blew a whistle and all of the clown fleas made it back in the carriage and were taken off stage. The circus was so entertaining that Constance and Titus completely lost track of time. Finally, Titus asked the cocker spaniel sitting next to him what time it was. The spaniel pulled a gold pocket watch out of his vest and said it was noon.

"We better get going," Titus said to Constance. "We have already been here over an hour. Riley must be waiting."

Titus and Constance went out the back of the tent, which was next to the river. Riley was waiting for them with the canoe in the water, filled with supplies. Riley had purchased an old wooden canoe.

"We have to hurry," Riley told Titus and Constance as all three entered the canoe.

The group started paddling and the canoe began to move forward. Riley continued, "I just left the general store and I think I saw the mean dogs. I was carrying the canoe over my head so all I could see were their paws, but I know it was them because one had a crutch. The group was asking around about a couple of real-worlders, and a gossipy old Pomeranian said she overheard the real-worlders saying they were going to the flea circus."

The group kept paddling, directing the canoe around a bend in the river. Suddenly, the group heard someone yell, "There they are!"

It was the terrier. Luckily the canoe went around a bend, making it harder for the dogs to reach them. The pit bull and the others in the dog pack wanted to run after the canoe, but the terrier suggested that they go and steal a boat to follow them. The terrier spotted an old rowboat tied to a dock and when no one was looking, the pack of dogs climbed into the boat and cut the boat free from the dock. By the time the dog pack got going, Riley, Titus and Constance had a big head start.

"This part of the river is pretty calm, but when we get around the next bend, it will speed up and we will have to make it through the rapids," Riley warned Titus and Constance.

"Titus, grab an oar and stay on the right side and paddle when the water is slow. When we start hitting the rapids, use the oar to keep us off the rocks. Constance, you do the same on the left side with the other oar. I will be in the back with the large pole steering the canoe."

As they rounded the bend, all they could see was white water, large rocks and rapids. Titus gulped.

"Are you sure this is a good idea?" asked Titus.

"Well, you came to Dreamland for adventure, so now you are about to have a mighty big one," Riley responded.

Right before they turned the corner, Riley saw the dog pack following them in an old wooden boat.

"Looks like the mean dogs couldn't find a canoe, so they got an old rowboat instead. I didn't see any oars which make me think they don't know anything about boating or about this river," said Riley.

Sure enough the boat, loaded down with too many dogs, was rounding the bend in the river when the pit bull saw the first rapids. He started barking and howling, but with no oars, they could not turn back.

Riley directed the canoe around several boulders, and Titus and Constance paddled hard to keep the canoe heading the right direction. Soon, they were through the first set of rapids and were picking up speed.

"I think the first waterfall is up ahead. Keep the canoe steering straight. When we start going over the waterfall, sit on the bottom of the canoe, lean back and hold on tight," Riley instructed.

Somehow, the boat with the dogs made it through the rapids and was floating sideways on the calm water. But just when the dogs thought they were safe, the terrier spotted the back of the canoe with the real-worlders rise up in the air and disappear over a waterfall. Everyone in the dog boat started to yelp and a few jumped into the water, trying to dog paddle to the shore. The rest were paddling on both sides, trying to steer the boat away towards the shore, but all they did was keep the boat in the center of the river.

Titus, Constance and Riley all screamed loudly as the canoe headed over the waterfall. The canoe plummetted down the fall before it landed upright on the river below. Riley looked back and saw the mean dogs' boat hit the bottom of the first waterfall, without any of the dogs in the boat. He looked around for the dogs and saw one dog after another go over the waterfall, waving their paws in the air as if they were trying to fly. One dog was even trying to dog paddle back up the waterfall.

Titus went to catch his breath but before he could, the canoe went over another waterfall. This one was even taller than the first.

"Hold on!" shouted Riley to his friends. They were about to go over the largest waterfall of them all. With everyone in the canoe holding on for dear life, the canoe went over the waterfall and seemed to be suspended in the air forever. When the canoe hit the river, it and all of its passengers sank right to the bottom of the river. The canoe appeared stuck in the sand, but luckily with a bit of rocking, the canoe surfaced, and the group paddled to shore to catch their breath.

Once ashore, the group saw the dogs' boat go over the waterfall. When it hit the water, it broke into tiny pieces. Thankfully, there was no sign of the dogs, so Riley assumed all the dogs were either onshore or stuck on rocks.

While Riley was pulling the canoe out of the water, Constance noticed a colony of beavers come out from a dam off the side of the river. They were collecting the broken pieces of wood.

One of the larger beavers came over and introduced himself. "Hi, my name is Avery." He looked at their canoe and said, "Are you guys crazy! You can't canoe down the Hunter River!"

"We are heading to Bounty Bay, and from looking at a map, this was the fastest way to get there," said Riley.

"Your map must be old," said Avery. "This river has been impassable by boat ever since I can remember. As a matter of fact, the next waterfall is twice as tall as the one you just came down, and after that, there are miles of white water rapids. If the waterfall doesn't get you, the rapids will. You were very lucky to get this far," Avery added.

"Is there a path we can take to get to Bounty Bay?" Constance asked.

"Yes. Just follow the river, pass by a couple of backcountry towns and eventually you will end up at Bounty Bay," Avery said.

"We also have a slight problem," Titus added. "There are some mean dogs following us. They will probably be on foot given that the wood you're collecting is what is left of their boat," Titus said, pointing to the wood.

"First, we need to hide your canoe so they don't know you are on foot," said Avery. Avery called some of the beavers over and within a minute, they had chewed the canoe into pieces and brought the scraps to their home in the dam.

"Why don't you all follow me to our home and we can have lunch while the dogs make their way down the path," Avery suggested. "This way, the dogs will be in front, and they won't be looking behind for you."

Everyone took a deep breath and dove underwater until they were under the dam. When they surfaced, they were in a beautiful home with several bedrooms, a kitchen and a large dining room. Avery brought them fresh fish, berries and a large spring salad. On one side of the table sat Riley, Titus and Constance. On the other side were Avery and six other beavers. Running around the dining room floor were a bunch of baby beavers chewing on twigs and hitting a ball back and forth with their tails.

At first, Titus was going to make up a story as to why they were being chased by the mean dogs, but then he remembered what happened to Squirrely when he lied, so he told Avery the whole story about the map, Mrs. Harriet's Boarding House, the parrot and the dogs.

When the story was done, Avery pushed his chair back a bit and said, "Don't worry, you can have all the treasure. It means nothing to a beaver. We have everything we need, and the treasure would only bring us trouble."

Avery paused to listen to something outside. The group could hear the mean dogs barking and blaming each other for losing the boat and almost drowning. The terrier suggested that the dogs make their way to the shore and follow the shoreline to Bounty Bay. He thought it would be easier than trying to follow the river. The group heard the dogs bark in agreement and then listened to the sounds of twigs breaking as the dogs made their way down the hill.

"That's some good luck," said Avery. The river path is a bit harder, but a lot shorter and faster. "Do you know exactly where the treasure is buried?" asked Avery.

"Yes," said Titus. He pulled the map out of his vest, but it was dripping wet. When he opened it up, all of the ink had smeared together and the map was ruined.

"Now what are we going to do?" asked Titus, upset. "The map is ruined and we don't know where the treasure is hidden."

"Yes, we do," said Constance. "Remember, I made a copy and gave it to Evie so she would know where to meet us. All we have to do is to get to Bounty Bay and hope our ship is there waiting for us."

Meanwhile, their ship had just left Wolf Dog Harbor and was making its way to Bounty Bay. Evie and Millie were back in the crow's nest, keeping an eye out for rocks, islands and other ships. Evie used this time to get Millie caught up about Riley, Titus, Constance, the treasure map and the mean dogs.

Evie pulled the map out of her vest to show Millie where the treasure was buried when a large gust of wind tore the map out of Evie's hands. Evie screamed, "The map!" Her scream was so loud that Harper and Remy both looked up at the same time to see the map slowly floating down towards the sea.

Before anyone could react, Millie grabbed the closest rope and jumped off the crow's nest. As she descended, she swung out over the water and grabbed the map right before it hit the water. Harper and Remy pulled Millie back on board and Evie climbed down to thank Millie.

"I know this is only a copy, but you need to take better care of it," instructed Harper.

"Can you put it someplace safe in the captain's quarters?" asked Evie. "I don't want to be responsible for it anymore." Before putting it away, the group looked over the map to see where they should go.

"I think we should anchor here," Harper said, pointing at the map. "It is as close to the X as we can get with the ship. We will have to use a small boat to get to land, " Harper announced to the crew.

Evie was trying to remember what time she went to bed to see if they would get there before she woke up.

Back at the dam, Avery showed Riley, Titus and Constance the path. "Here is some water, food and a couple of ropes you may need to descend the waterfalls. With any luck, you should get there before the end of the day," Avery said.

With that, the group was off. The first obstacle was the very tall waterfall Avery had warned them about. The path along the waterfall was wet and slippery. Using the ropes, it took almost 30 minutes to get to the bottom of the falls. From then on, the path was pretty easy to descend. After a couple of more hours, they came to a lookout point where they could see Bounty Bay. Constance spotted the USS Puffin sailing into the bay, while Titus spotted the pack of mean dogs walking along the shore about 5 miles from Bounty Bay. Riley, Titus and Constance rushed down the path to get to Bounty Bay before the dog pack.

"Rats!" said Titus. "If the map didn't get ruined, we could have start digging for the treasure now and be out of here before the dogs arrive."

"It looks like that fishing boat is about to leave the bay to go fishing. Let's see if he will give us a ride out to the USS Puffin," Riley suggested. When they got to the dock, they asked the captain of the fishing boat for a ride out to the ship.

"Sure enough, hop in," said the captain of the fishing boat. The captain was a weather-worn old lab retriever with long gray whiskers and a pipe in his mouth. He was wearing a yellow slicker jacket and hat.

As Harper was dropping the anchor, he saw the fishing boat heading his way. At first, he thought it may be pirates, but then he saw Riley, Titus and Constance on the deck.

"Permission to come aboard?" Riley yelled up to Harper who looking down at the fishing boat.

"Permission granted!" Harper yelled down to Riley.

Soon the whole group was standing on the ship sharing stories of their latest adventures. Titus told everyone about meeting up with Riley and about the dangerous river. He also explained how the map got ruined by the waterfall and mentioned the nice beaver colony they met. He also told them that the mean dogs were following them and that they were probably on the shore of Bounty Bay by now.

Evie introduced the group to Millie and told them how Millie saved the copy of the map from being ruined by bravely grabbing onto a rope and swinging all the way down from the crow's nest to catch the map right before it landed in the ocean.

Riley, Titus and Constance each took turns introducing themselves and thanked Millie for rescuing the map.

Harper suggested they all go into the captain's quarters to look at the copy of the map and plan out the best way to get to the treasure without alerting the mean dogs.

Riley suggested that they go at night, get to the spot on the map, dig up the treasure and get it back to the ship before sunlight. Hopefully, the darkness would make it harder to be seen. Harper thought it was a good plan, but he was afraid the lanterns would attract the attention of the mean dogs.

Millie suggested they use the paper from the ruined map to draw a fake treasure map. They could leave it for the mean dogs as a distraction. That way, they could go during the day and take their time looking for the treasure since the mean dogs would be off looking for the treasure in the wrong place.

Everyone thought that was a good idea. Evie could sense she was about to wake up. She suggested that Remy, Millie, Harper and Riley work on the fake map while the kids were asleep in the real world, so the map would be ready when they returned.

CHAPTER 15

The Treasure

Good thing we are keeping a dream journal," said Titus. "So many things happen in our dreams that it would be hard to remember where to start our dreams when we fall asleep each night if we didn't write them down."

That night at dinner, Constance and Titus told their parents about Millie, the flea circus, the river, the waterfalls, the beaver colony and the mean dogs who were still following them. Constance mentioned Millie's plan on making a fake map so they could get the mean dogs off their trail and dig up the treasure that night.

Jack and Mrs. Drapkin were very interested in the story and were amazed at how detailed all their kids' dreams had been since Harper, Remy and now Millie joined their lives.

Soon, all the kids were tucked into bed and were putting their Dreamland animals to sleep in their own little matchboxes. Next thing they knew, they were back in the captain's quarters comparing the copy of the map to the fake map that Riley had drawn up with the help of Millie. Millie even added some drawings of pirate stuff around the edges.

"Wow, this looks better than the original," Constance said. "Anyone have a plan as to how to get the map to the mean dogs?"

"Since the mean dogs have never met Millie, maybe she should be the one to get the map to them," Titus said, thinking out loud. "She can go to the pack and tell them that she found the map near a waterfall and she wanted to see if the pack wanted to buy it," Titus added.

"That could be dangerous," said Harper. "What if they don't want to pay but offer her part of the treasure, and then make her go with them until the treasure is dug up? Once they find out they have been tricked, they may hurt her."

"I think I should go," said Riley.

"How will that work? They already know you and don't like you," Titus said.

"All I need to do is to walk by the pack close enough so they see me. Once they capture and search me, they will find the map. I will tell them that I stole the map from you and I was heading to find the treasure for myself. If they rush off to find the treasure, I will follow them to make sure they start digging and then I will try to stall them once they find the treasure isn't there. If they make me go with them, I will escape when they are digging for the treasure and join up with you," Riley suggested.

"Can anyone else think of a better plan?" asked Remy.

When no one could think of a better plan, Riley got ready to row ashore to meet the dog pack while the rest of the group got ready to go ashore to dig up the treasure.

"Someone will have to stay on board and guard the ship," said Remy. As much as Millie wanted to go seek the treasure, she volunteered to guard the ship. Evie decided she would stay and help Millie just in case the ship got attacked.

With that, the crew let down two small boats: one for Riley and one for Harper, Remy, Titus and Constance. Both boats headed for shore at the same time. Riley rowed to the north part of the bay and the others rowed to the south part where the real treasure was buried.

With Titus and Constance rowing, they got to the beach first. Everyone jumped out and pulled the boat ashore and hid it under some bushes growing near the shore.

"By the looks of it, we have about a two-mile walk to get to the treasure," said Titus.

Pulling the picks and shovels in a small wagon, they headed inland. The bushes had grown over the path that was marked on the map, so it took them a lot longer to get to the treasure than they planned.

Meanwhile, Riley headed to the place he last saw the mean dogs. Instead of being in a camp as he expected, the pack had found a small café and were sitting around the counter, eating, drinking and planning their next move. Riley was outside the café, so he could not hear what they were saying.

The café was open on all four sides. It was built of bamboo poles and palm leaves made up the roof. Inside the café was an old wooden counter made up of a bunch of abandoned wooden crates, and the counter was made from an old door, probably from a fishing boat.

"We know that they were heading towards Bounty Bay and we saw their ship anchored offshore," said the terrier. "We should split up. Half the pack attacks the ship, takes it over and searches for the map on board. Bulldog will go down to the beach and keep an eye out to see if the real-worlders show up. The rest of us will wait here until the real-worlders are spotted."

"Why do I have to go to the beach while you get to sit here and eat and drink?" whined the bulldog.

"Because I am in charge," barked the terrier using his big dog bark that made him sound as big as a German shepherd.

Riley walked by the café, taking no notice of the group, when the terrier yelled out, "Hey, that's the pup from the boarding house who dropped the steaks on my head. Let's get him!"

With that, the group went running out and the old greyhound caught up with him first and held him so the rest of the pack could get there. As Riley resisted, the map fell out of his vest onto the ground.

"What do we have here?" asked the terrier, picking up the map. "Take him behind the café so we can ask him some questions," the terrier said as he winked to the others.

Once they were behind the café, the terrier opened the map and could not believe his eyes. It was the treasure map!

"If you tell us how you got the map and why you are here, we will give you part of the treasure," the terrier offered with his paw crossed behind his back.

"If you guys want to help me find and dig up the treasure, I will give you half," Riley counter-offered.

"We have the map, so we don't need to give you anything," the terrier responded. "So, tell me how you got it and we will give you a small portion of the treasure."

"I can see that I am outnumbered and outsmarted," said Riley. "I will tell you what you want to know. After the real-worlders found the map, they climbed out of the window and headed towards Flea Town. I followed them there, and when they got a canoe and went down the river, I ran alongside using the footpath and kept an eye on them. At the last waterfall, they all went into the water and lost all their supplies as well as their canoe. As they were swimming to the opposite side of the river, I saw the map float ashore. I grabbed the map and ran off before they could see me. Last I saw of them, they were all searching for the map," Riley told them.

The greyhound stayed and guarded Riley while the rest of the pack moved out of hearing distance.

"Do you think he is telling the truth?" asked the bulldog.

"It makes sense," said the terrier. "Okay, here is the new plan. I want you four to go steal a boat, row out to the ship and capture it so we can sail away with the treasure. Bulldog, your new job is to go steal another boat and be ready to go when we return with the treasure. The rest of the pack will go and find the treasure and bring it back to the boat."

"What about the pup?" asked one of the pack.

"Take him with us, in case this is some kind of a trap. Once we find the treasure, we can decide what to do with him."

Four of the dogs went back to the café, finished their drinks, paid the waiter and headed to the beach. The rest of the group went back to where Riley was being guarded.

"We decided to trust you about the map. We are all heading there now and you will join us so we can make sure to give you part of the treasure," the terrier said in his nicest voice. Riley still didn't trust the terrier.

"What about those four; how come they aren't joining us?" asked Riley.

"Oh, they are going to the harbor to see if they can buy a ship, so we have something to sail off in once we find the treasure," lied the terrier.

Riley knew the pack didn't have enough money to buy a ship, so he had an uneasy feeling.

The pack followed the map up a dirt trail for a mile and then made a left onto a small goat trail. The trail was rarely used, so it was hard to walk on. The terrier thought this was a good sign because a treasure should be buried near an old trail, not a well-used one.

By this time Titus, Constance, Harper and Remy made it to where the X was on the map. Although there was a clearing in the jungle, there was no sign of an X on the ground. The group spent an hour looking for the X while Remy double- and triple-checked the map. The group decided to take a break and to sit down under a large palm tree. Titus climbed the tree and knocked down some coconuts to eat and they drank the coconut's milk.

"Watch out below!" yelled Titus as he started knocking down coconuts.

The group got up and moved so they wouldn't be hit in the head with a coconut. Just as Titus was about to climb down, he noticed a large rock off to the left of the clearing and what appeared to be an

150

X carved in the rock. From the ground, the rock was blocked by bushes, but from up in the tree, Titus could see it clearly.

"I think I found the location of the treasure," Titus yelled down as he was descending the tree.

Everyone dropped the coconuts they were collecting and followed Titus to the rock he spotted.

"That rock is too far away from the X on the map," Constance said.

"Don't forget we have a copy so there could be an error as to where the treasure is," Harper reminded Constance.

The four mean dogs stole a boat when no one was looking and started rowing out to the ship. Evie and Millie were eating lunch and talking, so they didn't notice the boat moving in their direction.

The terrier led the pack up a steep path that took them to a peak where they decided to rest.

"This seems like an odd place to bury a treasure," the terrier said. "How did they get the treasure up here and how are we going to get it down?"

No one said anything because they could tell the terrier was in a bad mood. After the rest, they climbed down the other side of the peak and found the spot where the X was marked on the map. The spot was overgrown with bushes, so it took the pack awhile to make a clearing. Once this was done, and they were ready to dig, the terrier realized he had forgotten to bring picks and shovels.

"Okay pup, if you want part of the treasure, start digging," ordered the terrier. The rest of the pack sat under a palm tree and rested.

Like most dogs, Riley was a pretty good digger. He started digging with his front paws and all the dirt went on the pack. The terrier yelled at Riley to throw the dirt the other way, so Riley turned around so the dogs wouldn't get hit.

Meanwhile, at the spot where the real treasure was, Titus and Constance started digging below the rock. They dug for a while, but being that it was midday, Titus and Constance grew hot and needed to take a break. Harper and Remy took their turns at digging. Soon, one of the picks hit something solid. At this point, everyone helped to clear the dirt from the top of what appeared to be an old wooden chest. With all the group's strength, they lifted the chest out of the hole and placed it under a palm tree.

As they were about to pry open the top of the chest to see the treasure, they heard small cannon fire from the bay. Titus quickly dropped his pick and climbed up the tree to see what was happening. What he saw was a small rowboat with four dogs heading towards his ship and Millie and Evie aiming a small cannon at the approaching boat.

"Looks like the mean dogs are attacking the ship!" Titus yelled down. "No time to open the chest. Let's put it in the small wagon and head down as fast as we can to help them."

With some effort, they were able to lift the chest into the wagon and start down to the beach.

Unfortunately, the terrier also heard the cannon.

"You keep digging. I am going up to the peak to see what all the noise is about," said the terrier. As soon as the terrier was out of sight, Riley said he needed a break. The greyhound ordered Riley to go down to the river and bring back water for everyone.

"I can see you from here, so don't try and escape," warned the greyhound.

Riley got to the river and started to fill up the bucket with water. Riley heard the terrier shout something and the greyhound turned his head to follow the sound. Acting quickly, Riley jumped into the river and started dog paddling towards Bounty Bay.

The terrier came rushing back down the peak and told the pack they had been tricked. He saw the real-worlders rowing out to the ship with a large treasure chest. He also saw the four dogs trying to bail out water from their rowboat, which had been hit by a cannon.

"Grab the pup and let's get down to the boat the bulldog stole so we can row out to the ship before they leave," the terrier ordered. "Where is the pup anyway?" the terrier asked the greyhound.

"He is down there getting water for everyone," said the greyhound as he pointed to the river where Riley should have been. But all he saw was a bucket as Riley had slipped away.

"We will take care of him later," said the terrier. "Let's hurry up and get to the boat before they set sail."

As the pack headed down, Harper, Remy, Titus and Constance rowed right past the four dogs in the boat. The boat was just about to sink when the dogs jumped overboard and started dog-paddling to shore.

Luckily for Riley, at this point in the river, there were no waterfalls or rapids. Riley made it to the beach in no time. On the beach was the boat the bulldog had stolen, but the bulldog was nowhere to be seen. Riley looked towards the café, and just as he thought, he could see the bulldog sitting at the counter with a drink in his paw, talking to a waitress.

Riley quickly pushed the rowboat into the bay and started rowing as hard as he could. He passed some of the dogs paddling back ashore, but they took no notice of him since they were doing everything they could to keep their heads above water.

The terrier and the dog pack ran by the café and saw the bulldog sitting at the counter.

"Where is the boat?!" the terrier screamed at the bulldog.

"It's right there on the beach," the bulldog said, pointing over his shoulder at the beach. When the bulldog turned around, he noticed the boat was gone.

"Go get me another boat now!" the terrier barked even louder. "They are getting away with our treasure."

While the bulldog was looking for another boat, the four other dogs made it ashore and were lying on the beach, trying to catch their breath.

The terrier could see that the real-worlders were already aboard the ship, and the treasure was being hoisted aboard. He let out a growl.

While the bulldog was looking for another boat, the terrier went up to a fisherman who was getting ready to head out to fish.

"Excuse me," he said to the captain. "You see that ship out there? Well, they have stolen our treasure, and if you help us recover it, I will give you a share."

"How big of a share?" asked the captain, interested.

"Really big," answered the terrier, lying.

"Okay," said the captain. "Hop in and we will set sail to the ship."

Once the ship was loaded, Harper ordered for the ship to set sail.

"What about Riley?" asked Constance. He was about halfway between the ship and the beach. He was rowing as fast as he could. Evie shouted down from crow's nest that the mean dogs were on a fishing boat, heading their way.

"At this rate, the fishing boat will get to us before Riley will. We need to leave now, or the mean dogs could board the ship before Riley makes it here," said Remy.

"But I promised Riley part of the treasure, and we can't break a promise," Titus told Remy.

Suddenly, Titus woke up and found himself back in his bed. "No, not now!" he yelled.

Titus looked at the clock and it was 2:00 a.m. He first went into Evie's room and then into Constance's room and saw they were both still sleeping. He jumped back into bed and in no time, he was asleep and back on board the ship.

"Where did you go?" asked Constance.

"I woke up, but when I saw what time it was, I went back to sleep," said Titus.

By this time, the fishing boat was closing in on Riley.

"Sail by that rowboat so we can pick up the pup," ordered the terrier. "He escaped us once before, but he won't get away this time."

"No," responded the old retriever. "This is my boat and I am the captain."

"Not anymore," the terrier said and ordered the bulldog to take the captain below.

The only problem with the terrier's plan was that none of the dogs knew how to sail a boat. As they started to overtake Riley, the wind picked up and the fishing boat started heading toward shore, which had several large rocks sticking out of the water.

The terrier realized his error and had the captain brought back on deck. The terrier apologized and offered the captain a larger share if he got them to the ship before they set sail.

By the time the captain avoided the rocks and got the fishing boat sailing in the right direction again, Riley had made it to the ship and was climbing on board. Now, Harper made the official call to set sail. The sails were raised and the ship picked up speed.

By now, it was clear that the fishing boat could not catch up to the ship, so the terrier asked the captain to stop near the boat Riley used, which was just floating in the water. All the dogs got into the boat and the terrier ordered the bulldog and the greyhound to row since they were the ones that let the treasure getaway. The mean dogs didn't even thank the captain.

Once the ship left Bounty Bay, everyone went to the captain's quarters to talk about where to go next.

Titus suggested they head to Ronsdale Village, which is where the kumons live.

"Since it is the southernmost part of Dreamland, from there we can work our way up the coast and back to Puffin Village," Titus suggested.

"What about Riley? He might not want to be away from his home for that long," Constance said.

Riley said that the boat would be sailing by Coonhound, which is on the tip of Sanderling Island. "That would be a good place to get more supplies and to drop me off." Riley continued, "Coonhound is a nice city, and it would be a good place to spend the day while the supplies are being loaded."

Everyone agreed and Remy set course for the Port of Coonhound.

"Now that the course is set, I think we should open the treasure chest and see what is in it," Harper suggested. They carried the chest out to the deck so Remy could watch. Remy was busy steering the ship. Both Evie and Millie swung down from the crow's nest and landed right in the center of the deck.

"That was very impressive," Constance said to Evie. "Where did you learn to do that?" she asked.

"From my new best friend, Millie," Evie said with an arm around Millie.

Titus got a pick and started swinging it at the lock on the chest. Soon, the lock was broken and Titus opened the chest. Before they could see what was in it, Evie yelled, "I think I am waking up!"

Everyone looked at her expecting her to disappear, but she started giggling and told them that she was just kidding.

They continued to open the chest and everyone took a deep breath. The chest was filled to the top with goodies: gold coins, pearls, diamonds, rubies, emeralds, gold candlestick holders and a beautiful gold crown crested with jewels from every part of Dreamland.

Everyone stared at the treasure.

"I think you now have enough treasure to go anywhere in Dreamland and buy anything you want," said Remy, her eyes wide.

"How about we give Riley his share and the rest stays at your house in Puffin Village," suggested Titus.

Everyone agreed, so Riley went below deck and got the first thing he could find to hold his portion of the treasure, which was an old pillowcase. He filled it with gold and jewels almost to the point that he could barely carry it. He left the crown and other large jewels in the chest. Even with the pillowcase full of treasure, the chest still looked full.

After Riley took his share, they carried the chest to the captain's quarters, and Remy suggested they have dinner. While dinner was being made, the kids woke up. It started with Constance and then Evie disappeared.

"Well, I guess I am next," said Titus with a wave. "We will meet you back on board before you dock in Coonhound." And with that, Titus disappeared too.

After rowing for what seemed to be hours, the terrier and the pack of mean dogs made it ashore.

"It looks like they sailed south," said the terrier. "I bet they are going to stop in Coonhound for supplies before they sail home. If we take the mountain ridge trail, we could get there before they leave."

The mean dogs agreed on the plan and went to the café for refreshments and a rest before they set off to Coonhound.

CHAPTER 16

Coonhound

So, how was your adventure in Dreamland last night?" asked Mrs. Drapkin as she and the kids were preparing dinner. Before they could answer, Jack walked in, said something smelled good and tried to take a piece of stuffing that Mrs. Drapkin was taking out of the turkey.

She playfully slapped his hand and asked, "What are you doing home early?"

"The boss let me go home early since sales were slow at the store. With such great weather, it seems people would rather spend time outside rather than go shopping," Jack said.

Jack added, "Tomorrow is bring your-kids-to-work day. Do any of you kids want to go to work with me?" he asked. Titus and Constance were very excited to go and said yes. Evie shook her head no. She would rather stay home and play with Millie.

"Great! I will wake you all at 6:00 a.m. That will allow you to get dressed and have breakfast," said Jack.

The kids became less excited at the mention of waking up early. Since it was nearly spring, they had gotten used to sleeping in. None of the kids said anything because they could see how happy their dad was that they wanted to go to work with him.

At dinner that night, Constance and Titus tried to cover everything that happened in their dream last night.

They told about how the fake map worked to get the mean dogs off their trail, how Evie and Millie used a cannon to save the ship and how they found the treasure and got it on board the ship.

Titus was especially excited to tell his parents about opening up the treasure chest and finding it full of gold coins, jewels and a beautiful crown, and how they were going to share it with everyone.

Finally, Constance told them about their plan to sail to the Port of Coonhound for supplies and to drop off Riley with his treasure.

As soon as dinner was over, the kids asked if they could go to bed early because they wanted to have a full night to spend in Dreamland since they would have to wake up early the next morning.

Jack and Mrs. Drapkin excused the kids, and they all quickly got ready for bed. Soon, all three of the kids were back on board the ship, sitting in the captain's dining room.

Remy and Riley were about to eat breakfast while Harper was steering the ship and Millie was up in the crow's nest.

"How come you guys usually show up when there is food being served?" Remy asked with a laugh. "Don't they feed you in the real world?"

"Of course, but it is our dream and we just love food," Titus said.

"Should I bring meals to Harper and Millie?" Evie asked.

"No, they both ate already," answered Remy.

While Riley was making food for everyone, Remy showed Titus and Constance where they were on the map.

"As soon as we get around this peninsula," Remy said, pointing at the map, "we will be entering the Port of Coonhound. If the wind keeps up like it is now, we should arrive in about an hour."

As everyone was eating their breakfast of pancakes, butter, blueberries and syrup, Titus asked what they missed while they were back in the real world. Remy told them that they didn't miss anything. Their trip was trouble-free and the weather was perfect.

The same could not be said for the mean dogs. The dog pack was slowly moving along the ridge trail, especially with the terrier having to walk with a crutch. At one of the rest stops, the Saint Bernard decided to make a saddle out of branches, so the terrier could ride on his back.

At first, the terrier refused because he was embarrassed to be traveling on the back of another dog, but he knew the faster they moved, the sooner they would reach the group and the treasure, so he gave up and hopped on the back of the Saint Bernard.

The terrier clicked his heels and said giddy-up, but the Saint-bernard stood on his back paws and threw the terrier to the ground.

"I'm not your horse, so you better not do that again," threatened the Saint Bernard. "I'm doing you a favor." The terrier got the point and didn't do it again.

Now the pack was making great time. They soon arrived at the last peak on the path where they could see Coonhound.

"Look," pointed the terrier. "There is the ship tied up at the wharf. If we hurry up, we can take over the ship, which surely has the treasure aboard and sail away."

"Who will sail the ship?" asked the bulldog. "We couldn't even sail the fishing boat."

"Good point, let me think," said the terrier. After a few moments, the terrier came up with a plan that he thought was foolproof. Since they were a pack of fools, it was hard to believe any plan the terrier would come up with would work.

With the ship tied up at the wharf, Riley suggested that they all go ashore. He wanted to check into a hotel and then he would show everyone around Coonhound.

"Don't you think we should leave someone on board to guard the ship?" asked Harper.

"Not necessary," answered Riley. "We left the pack of dogs back in Bounty Bay, and besides, you see that Doberman pinscher at the end of the wharf? His job is to guard the wharf and keep the ships safe."

With that, Riley took his pillowcase of treasure and everyone headed into town to sightsee and to buy supplies.

Coontown was surprisingly a beautiful town filled with colorful two-story buildings with large patios. In the center of town was a large old church with two bell towers. To their right was one of the largest hotels Titus and Constance had ever seen. They entered one of the buildings, and it was clear that it was a very expensive hotel.

Walking up to the front desk, a doorman dressed in a white uniform with brass buttons asked if he could carry the pillowcase for Riley, as he thought it was his luggage. Riley politely declined and went to the front desk.

A large old English springer spaniel dressed in a black pin-striped suit asked if Riley needed directions to a boarding house. He assumed Riley could not afford the hotel.

"No, thank you," said Riley. "I would actually like a room for a week." Riley didn't even ask for the cost.

"And how do you plan on paying for it?" asked the clerk, suspiciously.

Riley pulled out three gold coins from his pocket and dropped them on the counter. "Will this cover the cost?" asked Riley.

The clerk's voice changed from being suspicious to being friendly. "Yes, that will cover enough rooms for your whole group for the week," responded the clerk.

"No, it is just me," replied Riley.

The clerk clapped his hands together to summon the belldog and said, "Please take Mr. Riley to the Presidential Suite." Everyone wanted to know how the fancy room looked, so they followed the belldog.

On the second floor, the belldog opened the door to the suite at the end of the hall. The first thing the group noticed was the beautiful view of the harbor and the ocean. Next, they saw a large living room that had a couch, chairs and a white grand piano. Right next to the living room was a large dining room that would easily fit ten people.

The belldog brought Riley to the bedroom which had a king-size bed in the center and a fan over the bed. It also had a large bathroom off to the left with a bathtub and a shower.

"Welcome to your room," said the belldog. Riley handed the belldog a small silver coin, to say thanks. The belldog looked at the coin, bowed and left the room, closing the door behind him.

"This is amazing," said Constance. "How much is this going to cost?" she asked.

"Doesn't matter," responded Riley. "Thanks to you, I have enough treasure to live like this for the rest of my life."

After Riley put the pillowcase of treasure into the safe that was in the closet of the room, they all went out to explore the town. They went to the town center and past the large old church. As they walked to the fountain in the center of the square, the terrier spotted the group from his lookout point and told the pack that now was their chance to take over the ship.

The pack raced down the hill, and as they were about to get on the dock, they were stopped by the Doberman pinscher guard dog.

"Where do you think you're going?" asked the guard dog.

The terrier wasn't expecting to be stopped, so he didn't have a response ready.

"Uh, we are the crew of that ship over there," he said as he was pointing to the USS Puffin.

"Really?" questioned the guard dog, taking a closer look at the pack of dogs. He said, "You don't look like sailors. Prove to me that you are. What is the name of the center mast on the ship?" he asked as a test.

The terrier could not for the life of him remember the name. To stall, he asked, "Do you mean the main mast?"

The guard dog paused for a moment. "Correct," he responded. He moved out of the way so the group could pass and board the ship.

Once onboard, the terrier said, "Lucky us. That was a guess!" The terrier then told the group about his plan to steal the treasure.

"We go below deck and hide there until the ship is out to sea. Once we are far away from land, we pop out, surprise the group and take over the ship. We will steal their treasure and make them sail us back to Port Kaynine, where we will leave them empty-handed."

The pack thought it was a great idea and everyone went below deck and hid behind crates. The space was dark, wet, small and smelly, but it seemed like the best place to hide. No one would want to spend too long below deck because it did not smell good.

While the group was looking at the fountain in the town center, a horse and open carriage stopped at the group. The driver asked, "Would you like a tour of the town for $1.00?" The group thought that it would be a great way to see the town, so they agreed. Since there was only room for five, Harper and Remy offered to go get the supplies and prepare the ship for their trip. The rest of the group hopped on board for the tour of the town.

Harper and Remy went back towards the dock and spotted a ship supply store. Inside, they found everything that they needed for their trip and more. Since they had bought a lot of things, they borrowed a large wagon and horse to help bring the supplies to the ship. Harper and Remy loaded the supplies below the deck. They didn't see the pack of dogs hiding there, but Harper thought something smelled odd.

After a complete tour of the town, the carriage dropped the group off at the wharf. The group loved seeing the town and were surprised by all the expensive houses they saw.

Riley said, "I think I am going to stay in Coonhound and buy one of those fancy houses on the hill. Once I buy a house, I will let the hotel know where I am living so if you ever return, you can find me."

Everyone hugged Riley and promised to visit him in a future dream.

Just as Riley was about to leave, the guard dog welcomed the group back and told them that the two mice and the dog pack crew were on board the ship. "Best of luck for your journey," wished the guard dog.

"Wait a minute," asked Riley. "You said a dog pack crew was on board?"

"Yes," responded the guard dog. "They boarded about two hours ago, and I have not seen them since."

"Can you call the harbor police for us?" asked Riley. "That pack is not part of our crew."

"I thought they looked suspicious," answered the guard dog as he blew his whistle. "They didn't even help the mice load the ship. I should have known they were strangers."

Hearing the guard dog's whistle, five large German sheperds showed up wearing blue uniforms with matching blue caps and carrying large black batons.

The German shepherds followed the group to the ship and spoke with Harper and Remy to see what they knew.

"I think they may be hiding below deck," said Harper. "When we were loading supplies, it smelled like a wet dog down there."

All five German shepherds, followed by Titus, Constance, Harper and Remy descended the stairs to the hold. Riley decided to stay out of sight since he was planning on living Coonhound and he didn't want the mean dogs to come after him once they got out of prison.

The group started moving crates out of the way until they reached the very back of the hold. Sure enough, all the dogs were hiding in a corner soaked with water from a leaking plank in the side of the ship.

"You are all under arrest," barked one of the sheperds.

All the dogs were miserable hiding in the dark, cramped and wet hold, so they were almost happy to be arrested. The German shepherds guided the dogs off the boat and took them off to jail in the police wagon. Once they were gone, Riley came out from hiding.

"I guess you are ready to sail now that the mean dogs are gone," said Riley.

"Yes, we are going to sail the Ronsdale and work our way back to Puffin Village," said Titus. "Are you sure you don't want to join us?"

"No, I am going to spend the next few months buying a home and settling into my new life in Coonhound. You will come to visit me, right?" Riley asked.

"We will definitely come back," answered Constance. They all hugged and Riley jumped onto the dock and walked back into town.

Everyone prepped for their takeoff. Evie took a turn at the wheel while Millie was up in the crow's nest watching for rocks or other ships. Once they were in the open sea, Harper and Titus went into the captain's quarters to talk about their new destination.

It was going to be a two-dream journey to Ronsdale Village, so Remy took the wheel while Evie climbed up to the crow's nest so she could be with Millie.

Titus and Constance suggested to Harper that they find a good hiding place for the treasure just in case they run into any trouble on the voyage.

Titus remembered a book his dad used to read them. It was called *Treasure Island,* and there was a part when a boy hid in an apple barrel when the pirates came into the room.

"What if we took the apples out from the barrels, put the treasure at the bottom, then covered the treasure with the apples? That way if someone opens the barrels, it just looks like apples! If we throw the treasure chest overboard, no one will think the treasure is still here."

Everyone agreed. Once the barrel was emptied, they filled it with the treasure, topped it off with apples and brought the chest on deck. Next, they filled the chest with heavy items and dropped the chest overboard. The chest made a big splash when it hit the water. Soon, there was a loud bang and another big splash the near the ship.

"What was that?" asked Constance.

"Pirate ship off our port (left) side!" yelled Millie. "They just fired a cannonball at us, probably as a warning shot," she added.

Sure enough, there was a pirate ship approaching them from the east. "First the mean dogs, now pirates!" said Titus.

"We can't outrun them," said Remy, looking at the pirate ship. "Their ship is moving too fast."

The pirate ship pulled next to the USS Puffin and a few of the pirates threw grappling hooks to keep the two ships together.

"What is the meaning of this?" protested Harper.

The captain of the pirate ship was a colorful old parrot with an eye patch. He was wearing a three-pointed hat with a skull and crossbones in front. Titus noticed that all the pirate crew were colorful, but dirty, parrots.

Although the captain could just take over the ship now that they were tied together, he wasn't sure it was the ship he was looking for, so he decided to be polite.

"Permission to come on board?" asked the parrot captain.

"Please state your name and your purpose," Harper replied.

"My name is Captain Paulie. I am the captain of this fine vessel called the Flying Parrot, and I would just like to parlé, I mean talk," the captain responded in a heavy French accent.

"You can come aboard alone. But once aboard, you need to remove the grappling hooks. When we are finished speaking, you can fly back to your ship," said Harper.

"How about also allowing my first mate aboard too?" Captain Paulie asked. Harper agreed, and once aboard they unhooked the grappling hooks and the ships drifted apart.

Harper, Titus, Constance, the captain and his first mate all went to the captain's quarters and sat down.

"State your business," demanded Harper, trying to sound tough.

"I see you are a mouse who gets directly to business, so I will too," responded Paulie. "I was told by a little birdy that a few real-worlders found Captain Kidd's treasure. Since you have real-worlders aboard, I thought I would stop by and ask if you happen to know anything about the treasure."

"Feel free to search the ship," said Harper. "We have nothing to hide."

The captain and the first mate went over the ship from top to bottom. The first mate even took an apple out of the barrel and ate it while he was searching.

While the ship was being searched, Evie and Millie were keeping an eye on the pirate ship near them. Evie noticed that some of the gun ports were open and the cannons were being rolled into firing position.

Evie climbed down from the crow's nest and whispered into Titus' ear about the cannons being moved to the firing position.

After searching the complete ship, the captain and first mate went back to the captain's quarters.

"Looks like you may not be the real-worlders we are searching for," Paulie said. "I guess we will go back to the ship."

"Not so fast," said Titus, blocking the door. "How come you have rolled your cannons out to firing position?"

"Oh that. The crew always does that whenever I go aboard another ship," Paulie said somewhat unconvincingly.

"I'll tell you what," said Titus, "I will let your first mate return to your ship and once the cannons are pulled in and your ship is a mile away, I will let you fly back to the ship."

"Now, that's not very friendly," said Paulie. "We searched your ship and admitted we made a mistake. Now you want to keep me from leaving?!"

"To be more accurate, your ship pulled alongside our ship and is pointing loaded cannons at us," Titus responded.

"Well, to be even more accurate," Paulie said as he held up a pearl necklace, "I think you have lied about having Captain Kidd's treasure. So, if you hand the treasure chest over, we will leave and not bother you anymore."

Titus paused to think. Somehow, the necklace must have been dropped on the deck when they transferred the treasure to the apple barrels.

"That is not true," responded Titus. "You didn't ask if we had the treasure chest. You asked if you could search our ship, and we said yes."

Captain Paulie had to think about that for a minute. He had the pearl necklace in his pocket and pulled it out to make it seem like he found it while searching, hoping they would confess to having the treasure chest.

"Okay Titus, you seem like an honest young man. I'll tell you what. I will ask you three questions, and if you answer them honestly, we will leave your ship and promise not to bother you again," offered Captain Paulie.

Titus didn't really trust pirates, especially this one, but he thought that this may be the best way to get rid of the pirates without a fight, so he agreed.

"The first question is, did you or anyone in your group find Captain Kidd's treasure map?" asked Paulie.

To the pirate's surprise, Titus told them yes, they did find the map.

Bobbing his head side to side in delight, Paulie asked his second question; "Did you or any of your group find Captain Kidd's treasure chest?" Again to the surprise of the pirates, Titus said yes.

The pirate was happy with the way these questions were going. He asked his third question. "Where is the treasure chest now?"

"It's at the bottom of the sea, in Davy Jones' locker," responded Titus. "We dropped it overboard right before you arrived."

At this point, Paulie let out a loud screech. "Noooo!" Paulie did see a large splash before they fired the warning shot, so he knew Titus was telling the truth. Paulie assumed that Titus saw the pirate ship coming towards them and threw the chest overboard to avoid trouble from the pirates.

"I did see the splash, so it appears you have been honest. The first mate and I will fly back to our ship and leave you alone," said Paulie.

Titus moved away from the door and the two pirate parrots went on deck. Before flying away, Titus heard Paulie tell the first mate to ready the ship to return to the spot where the treasure chest was dropped overboard. The captain also told his first mate to ready the shags for diving. Shags are special birds that can dive up to 150 feet below the surface. With that, they flew back to the ship, and the ship slowly changed course.

"That was close," said Constance. "I was wondering how you were going to answer Paulie's questions without lying."

"Not telling the full story is a form of lying," responded Titus. "I knew Paulie wanted the treasure, not the treasure chest. I could have corrected Paulie and told him where the treasure is, instead of the treasure chest. However, because I was dealing with pirates who have no honor, I didn't feel it was necessary to add information to his questions. Now, let's get out of here before the pirates find there are rocks in the treasure chest and not treasure."

Just as the group was about to sail away, Titus and Constance were shaken awake by Jack.

"Hey, kids, time to get up and dressed. It's bring-your-kids-to-work day!" Jack said with a cheery voice.

Titus and Constance wanted to go to work with their dad, but they would have preferred to stay in Dreamland longer. Since Evie wasn't going to the toy store, she got to stay on board for a little while longer.

CHAPTER 17

Corny Island

While Titus and Constance were eating breakfast and then getting dressed, Jack took his new Sears Motor Buggy out of the garage and warmed the engine up. Jack recently ordered the horseless carriage for $395 from his Sears catalog. Although the car only had 10 horsepower, it could get up to 25mph on a downhill stretch of the road.

Once everyone was ready, they all hopped into the front seat and were off to Boise. Their ranch was in the foothills, so it was about 20 minutes from the town of Boise. With the Sears buggy being new, Titus and Constance loved going for a drive in it. Going 25mph was faster than they had ever gone before, and they loved the feeling of the wind in their hair.

Even though Titus and Constance left Dreamland to go to work, Evie and Millie were still on board the ship up in the crow's nest as usual. Using her toy telescope, Evie scanned the horizon for any ships or islands.

"Land ho," shouted Evie. Harper looked up to see Evie pointing off the bow of the ship. Harper went to the captain's quarters and looked over the map. There were no islands charted in this location. Harper decided to get a closer look, so he told Remy to keep the heading straight, which would get them into the bay in a few hours. Before Harper could tell Evie the plan, she woke up.

The toy store was located on the corner of 6th and Main. Jack parked his buggy in front of the store between two hitching posts for tying up horses. Although the sidewalks were paved, Main Street was still a dirt road. There was a trolly track right down the center, which Titus, Constance and Mrs. Drapkin used to get to the ice cream shop down the street when the family came into town to see Jack at the store or to go shopping.

Jack was the first person at the store that morning, so it was his job to open the store. He had to light the gas lamps and count the money in the cash register. Although the store did not officially open until 9:00 a.m., with the help of Titus and Constance, Jack opened the store a little bit early since there were a couple of parents and kids outside looking in the store window.

The store was not large, but it was packed to the ceiling with everything a kid would want. There were sections of dolls, stuffed animals, games, sporting goods and toy models. Titus's favorite part was the toy train section, while Constance liked playing in the doll section.

As Jack was talking to the parents, the two boys who were waiting outside walked around the store. The tallest of the two asked if Titus worked in the store. Titus said he was too young to work there but hoped to work in the store when he got older. He told the boys it was bring-your-children-to-work day at the store.

"Hi, my name is John," the taller boy said, walking over to Titus, "and this is my younger brother Pete."

"My name is Titus, and that girl over there is my sister Constance and my dad's name is Jack."

"Titus, you are so lucky to have a dad who works in a toy store. My dad works in a Jasper mine, so all he brings home are pretty rocks," John said. "Does your dad bring home lots of toys to play with often?"

"Not usually, but from time to time, he designs toys and then we get to play with them," Titus responded.

"My parents are looking for a toy for Pete and me to take with us on our train trip to Chicago to visit our relatives. What is your favorite toy?" John asked.

Titus, acting as if he really did work at the store, said, "Follow me."

John and Pete followed Titus over to the stuffed animal section and stopped in front of a display filled with Harper, Remy and Millie toys.

Titus picked up a matchbox that had a Harper stuffed animal inside. He opened the matchbox and gently lifted Harper out of the box.

"You still play with stuffed animals?" asked Pete.

"This isn't just any stuffed animal; this is a dream starter," answered Titus.

"Looks like a stuffed animal to me," said Pete.

Titus told John and Pete about Dreamland and how Harper helps him to get to Dreamland almost every night. He told them about some of the adventures and about some of the towns and islands Constance and Evie had visited. He mentioned that Constance had a Remy toy and Evie had a Millie as their Dreamland friends.

"So, if we get Dreamland friends, will we meet you in Dreamland?" asked John.

"I don't think it works that way," said Titus. "I think everyone has their own dream, and so far, we have been to Dreamland around fifteen times and we have yet to run into other real-worlders."

"What are real-worlders?" asked Pete.

"All the animals in Dreamland call us real-worlders since we live in the real world and we only visit Dreamland when we sleep," answered Titus.

With that, John took a Harper stuffed animal and Pete took a Remy stuffed animal to their parents at the counter and interrupted Jack to ask their parents if they could buy Harper and Remy for their trip to Chicago.

While the parents were surprised that the boys would want stuffed animals instead of games for the trip, they were happy since Harper and Remy came in nice matchboxes, which would be easy to pack for the trip.

Jack told the parents how Harper and Remy had made it so much easier to get the kids in bed and to get them to go to sleep without a fuss. Jack also told them about the book he was reading to the kids each night, which made it easy for the kids to have pleasant dreams instead of nightmares.

John's parents not only purchased a Harper and Remy for the boys but also purchased another five Harper, Remy and Millie stuffed animals to give to all the nieces and nephews in Chicago.

After the sale was made and the stuffed animals were wrapped in butcher paper, Jack complimented Titus on what a great little salesman he was. Jack gave Titus a quarter and told him that he and Constance could go over to the ice cream store and each buy ice cream.

Titus and Constance caught the trolly and hung on the outside since the trip was short. They jumped off in front of Mr. Morton's Ice Cream Parlor.

Inside the parlor, there was ice cream in large wooden tubs to the left where you select the ice cream you want. There was also a soda fountain and counter on the other side where you could sit to eat your ice cream or order a soda.

Titus ordered a root-beer float with vanilla ice cream, while Constance got carried away and ordered a banana split with strawberry, chocolate and vanilla ice cream. She also covered it with chocolate syrup, whipped cream and a cherry.

"That will be twenty cents for the rootbeer float and the ice cream sundae," said Mr. Morton.

After enjoying their ice creams, Titus and Constance decided to walk back to the toy store.

Mrs. Melville waved hi to the two kids as they were approaching her fruit and vegetable store. Titus stopped to talk with Mrs. Melville and with his extra nickel, he bought a big juicy apple for his dad.

When they returned the toy store, Mr. McGraw, the owner of the store, was in the back room working on an adding machine while Jack was helping a customer. Titus picked up a broom and started sweeping, while Constance got a feather duster and dusted all the beautiful porcelain dolls.

After a while, Mr. McGraw came out of the backroom and saw Titus and Constance hard at work.

"Do you kids want a summer job when you get old enough?" he asked Titus and Constance. "You kids are hard workers."

"Thank you for the offer," said Titus, "but It maybe a couple of years before we are old enough to work!"

At the end of the day, Jack locked up the store and they all headed home. Mrs. Drapkin, with the help of Evie, had dinner set on the table. After everyone washed up and prayers were said, Jack lifted the large platter of sliced pot roast and passed it around the table.

"How was work today?" asked Mrs. Drapkin.

"Titus and Constance helped a lot in the store," answered Jack, "and Titus made the biggest sale of the day."

"Yes and Mr. McGraw even offered Constance and me jobs, once we get older," said Titus.

Constance thought this was a good time to tell the family about last night's dream. She got her dream journal and told everyone about how beautiful Port Coonhound was, about the fancy houses and hotel, about the mean dogs hiding in the hold of the ship and about the guard dog calling the German shepherd police dogs that arrested the mean dogs and took the pack to jail.

Titus added that Riley took his share of the treasure and that Riley planned on buying a beautiful house and settling down in Coonhound. Titus also told them about the pirate parrots trying to steal the treasure and how they tricked the pirates into believing the treasure was thrown overboard with the treasure chest.

Evie added, "I saw an island." This didn't mean anything to Titus or Constance as they didn't know what she was talking about.

"Maybe you can use tonight's dream to explore the island," Jack suggested.

"If it is on the way to Ronsdale, then I am sure we can stop and check it out," said Constance.

Evie nodded.

Titus and Constance were tired from getting up early and working in the store, so after dinner, they asked if they could be excused. Constance helped clean the table while Titus took a shower. After his shower, Titus helped Mrs. Drapkin with drying the dishes while Constance took a bath.

Finally, they were all in bed when Jack went by and thanked Titus and Constance for helping out at the store. "It is great having children that willingly help out without having to be told what to do." Next, he went into Evie's room and gave her a big hug and put out all but one of the candles.

Soon, all the kids were back on board the ship. Evie climbed up to the crow's nest to be with Millie, and Constance and Titus went to the captain's quarters to find out about the island.

"This map is relatively new and it does not show an island anywhere near where we are," said Harper.

Just then Evie yelled, "Island dead ahead!"

Titus went up on deck with Harper's telescope to study the island. He only saw caves and there was no sign of houses or any inhabitants.

Titus returned and told Constance and Remy that it appeared to be a deserted island.

After the ship dropped anchor in the harbor, Titus, Constance, Harper and Remy rowed ashore while Evie and Millie kept an eye on the ship.

Titus pulled the dinghy onto the beach and everyone jumped out. Walking around, they saw no sign of life.

"I think I should claim this island. I will call it Titusville," said Titus.

From behind a rock came a hedgehog who asked, "What did the mother bee say to the baby bee?"

Titus turned around to see a cute little hedgehog standing there waiting for an answer.

"I don't know," responded Titus. "What did the mother bee say to the baby bee?"

"Beehive yourself," responded the hedgehog. The hedgehog fell on the ground from laughing so hard at his own joke.

"That is a pretty corny joke," said Titus.

"That's why this is called Corny Island," the hedgehog said, trying to hold back another laugh.

"My name is Mr. Clayton, and I am the mayor of Corny Island. Whenever you meet hedgehogs here, they will tell you a joke as their way of greeting you.

"Follow me, but make sure you lower your head when you enter," said Mayor Clayton.

Once they entered the hole, which was blocked by the rock, they discovered a huge underground city.

The ceiling had a large skylight in the center and was over ten stories high. On the ground level were streets and shops and all around the walls on the upper level were doors and windows that looked like small apartments. These apartments were on every level all the way up to the top. They saw kids running around the walkways in front of the apartments and mothers hanging out laundry.

Mayor Clayton walked the group down the main street and stopped in front of the mayor's office.

A little hedgehog, who had never seen real-worlders, got up enough courage to talk to Constance.

"Hi, my name is Abbey. What is the worst animal you can play cards with?" asked Abbey.

"A card shark?" asked Constance.

"No," said Abbey. "A cheetah!"

"Wow, these jokes are bad," whispered Titus to Remy.

When they entered the mayor's office, they were greeted by a little lady hedgehog is a blue dress.

"Hi, my name is Ava. I am Mr. Clayton's assistance. Can I get you something to drink?" After everyone ordered something to drink, Ava asked, "Why did the dog go to court?"

This time Harper said, "I don't know."

"Because he got a barking ticket," Ava said laughing as she walked away to get the drinks.

"When did you start the tradition of telling corny jokes?" asked Titus.

"One day, everyone seemed bored. With living underground, we always have the same weather and we hardly ever get visitors. So, we decided to make up jokes to tell each other whenever we meet, and it makes people laugh or at least smile," said Mayor Clayton.

Titus thought to himself that the bad jokes are more likely to get you to roll your eyes or wince than laugh, but he liked the concept.

Ava brought Mrs. Clayton into the office. "Dear, remember we are supposed to meet the Alrons for lunch today." He paused when he saw the group. "Oh, I didn't notice you had guests."

Mr. Clayton introduced Titus, Constance, Harper and Remy to Mrs. Clayton, and Mrs. Clayton asked, "What do you get when a chicken crosses the street, rolls in the mud and crosses the street again?"

Titus, Constance, Harper and Remy all responded at the same time, "I don't know, what do you get when a chicken crosses the street, rolls in the mud and crosses the street again?"

"A dirty double-crosser." And with that, Ava, Mayor Clayton and Mrs. Clayton all laughed so hard that the mayor accidentally blew some of his drink through his nose.

"I don't think I can take much more of this," Remy whispered in Titus' ear. "These jokes are pretty bad."

"Well, we don't want to keep you from lunch," Remy said, standing up.

"Why don't you join us?" asked Mrs. Clayton.

"Thank you for the offer, but we are on our way to Ronsdale and we spotted your island, so we thought we would stop and explore because it was not on our map and we wanted to see what's here," said Remy.

"Yes, our island was removed from all maps ever since the first explorers stopped in. I think it was because they didn't find our jokes funny. They thought they would save others from having to hear them by leaving us off the map," responded Mayor Clayton. "Do you think our jokes are funny?" he asked the group.

Everyone looked at each other. Then Titus responded, "We have never heard anything like the jokes you tell here on Corny Island," Titus said, smiling.

Just then, Kyle walked into the room. Kyle was the youngest son of the Claytons.

"Kyle, this is Titus, Constance, Harper and Remy. Can you show them around a bit and then show them the way back to their ship?" asked Mayor Clayton.

"Sure, Dad," Kyle responded. Then he asked, "What did the porcupine say to the cactus?"

Titus, Constance, Harper and Remy all spoke at the same time, "I don't know, what did the porcupine say to the cactus?"

"Are you my mother?" Kyle responded. "Get it because they both have spikes!" Everyone laughed or pretended to.

"With that, I think we should be leaving," Harper said. "It was great meeting you all, and we promise not to add your island back on the map," Harper said.

On the way to the ship, they walked past several shops, and when they got to the bakery, it smelled so good that Remy decided to go in to buy some fresh bread for the journey.

After Remy placed an order for six loaves of bread, the baker asked, "How do you catch a squirrel?"

Titus, Constance, Harper and Remy all said at the same time, "I don't know, how do you catch a squirrel?"

"Climb up a tree and act like a nut," the baker responded. All the customers in the store started to laugh.

With the loaves of bread in hand, the group managed to make it to the beach without having to talk to any more of the Cornyians. After rowing out the ship, they set sail for Ronsdale.

Harper, Constance and Titus were in the captain's quarters looking over the map when Titus asked, "What time is it when you arrive at Corny Island?"

Tired of hearing bad jokes, Harper and Constance rolled their eyes and asked at the same time, "I don't know, what time is it when you arrive at Corny Island?"

"Time to leave," said Titus and everyone laughed.

Evie and Millie, up in the crow's nest, spotted a white pigeon heading towards the ship.

"Isn't that kind of unusual having a pigeon this far from the mainland?" asked Evie.

Before Millie could respond, the pigeon landed on the rail around the crow's nest and lifted a leg that appeared to have a small paper tied to it. Evie undid the ribbon which held the paper on and unrolled it to see that there was a message written in very formal handwriting.

Even in Dreamland, Evie couldn't read yet, so she grabbed a rope and swung down to the deck where Titus and Constance were talking to Remy.

"A pigeon just delivered this message," said Evie, slightly out of breath from swinging down so quickly.

"It's from Milo, the kumon I met on the train to Willets," said Titus.

"What does it say?" asked Constance and Evie at the same time.

Titus read the message:

Dear Mr. Titus,

We need your help. Someone has stolen our Supreme Book. This book is very important because it contains all the histories of Ronsdale Village. As avid book readers, kumons treasure this book more than all the riches in Dreamland. With your reputation as a famous badger fighter and detective, we need your help to recover the book. Please make your way to Ronsdale Village as fast as possible, and meet me at my treehouse, which is located at the corner of Park Ave and Oak St.

From Milo

"Famous badger fighter and detective?" Constance questioned Titus.

"Well, the badger fighter comes from the badgers who were trying to rob the train to Willets. We defeated them by crashing through the large log they had placed on the tracks," Titus said. "And I guess the famous detective comes from finding the treasure map."

Titus got a piece of paper and wrote:

Milo,

My trusted partner Constance and I will be there tomorrow to help recover the Supreme Book.

Your friend Titus.

"Evie, please tie this to the pigeon's leg quickly because I think we will be waking up soon," asked Titus.

Just when Evie made it back to the crow's nest and tied the message to the pigeon, she disappeared.

"Harper, you, Remy and Millie sail as fast as possible to Ronsdale Village, and we will meet you on board when we return to Dreamland," Titus said. Before Remy could respond, Titus and Constance woke up.

CHAPTER 18

Ronsdale Village

That evening, Constance told her parents about Corny Island and about the bad jokes everyone told. Constance said that those jokes made her dad's jokes seem funnier now that she knew what bad jokes really sound like.

Titus told his parents about the mysterious message he received from Milo at Ronsdale Village, and how Milo wanted him and Constance to help find the missing Supreme Book which had the whole history of Ronsdale Village written in it.

"Titus, do you remember the book I read to you and Constance awhile back about the great detective Sherlock Holmes and his partner Dr. Watson?" asked Jack.

"Yes, Sherlock Holmes was the best detective ever!" responded Titus.

"Well, why don't you and Constance show up in Ronsdale Village dressed like Holmes and Watson?" suggested Jack.

That night before bed, Titus and Constance took the *Adventures of Sherlock Holmes* off the bookshelf and looked at some of the illustrations so they would know what to wear for tonight's dream.

When they returned to Dreamland that evening, the ship was just pulling into Ronsdale Harbor. Titus was wearing a hat just like the one Sherlock Holmes used to wear. He also had a long wool coat, a pipe in his mouth and a large magnifying glass in his hand. Constance was wearing a gray wool suit with a matching vest and a black bowler hat. Evie didn't know anything about Sherlock Holmes, so she returned in her light blue sailor dress she had been wearing ever since they stopped dressing as pirates.

After tying up at the dock, the group made their way into town. Evie and Millie decided to stay aboard and keep an eye on the ship in case the pirate parrots caught up to them. Evie said she would ring the ship's bell three times if there was any trouble.

Except for a few ship supply stores and a grocery market near the dock, there were no other buildings in Ronsdale.

When Titus saw a kumon walking past, he asked, "Excuse me. How do you get to Park Ave and Oak Street?"

The kumon asked Titus if he was the famous detective who was going to find the Supreme Book. Titus nodded, so the kumon told Titus that he was already on Park Ave. If he went straight past the first intersection, he would be at Park Ave and Oak Street. That was where Milo lived.

Remy and Harper said they would go shopping for supplies and would meet them there later. Constance, who had never seen a kumon, was surprised how this kumon looked just like a mixture of a tabby cat and a Yorkshire terrier.

When Titus and Constance got to Park and Oak, all they saw were rolling hills of golden grass and huge oak trees. Titus noticed that on one of the oak trees was a sign that said *Milo Pepper* near what looked like a door knocker. Titus used the door knocker and soon a door in the tree opened, and Milo was standing there with a big smile.

"You made it," said Milo, clearly happy to see them. "Please come up to my treehouse."

After climbing a winding staircase for quite a while, they found themselves if a very spacious room. When they walked to the balcony, they looked out to see that every oak tree was really a treehouse.

Milo asked Titus and Constance to join him at the table. There was a pitcher of fresh milk that Milo poured into saucers in front of Titus and Constance. Titus guessed that because they liked milk in saucers, kumons were more cat than dog. After everyone leaned forward and lapped up the milk with their tongues, Milo got directly to business.

"The largest oak tree in the center of town is our library," Milo said while pointing to the tall old oak in the town center. "The Supreme Book is kept in a locked cabinet behind the librarian's desk. Or so it was until someone stole it."

"Who was the last person to check out the book?" asked Titus.

"Young Todd checked it out three days ago as a reference for a school report he is working on," responded Milo.

"Does Ronsdale Village have any enemies who may want to steal the book?" asked Constance.

"Well yes. The kittens of Ploverville have always been jealous of kumons," replied Milo. "They are only kittens or cats, and we are a combination of puppies and kittens.

"We are convinced that the dreaded kittens of Ploverville have our book and our mayor was about to go to Ploverville and demand our book back. But when I suggested that we have Titus and Constance, the great detective team, come here first to make sure the kittens stole the book, the mayor agreed to wait before going to Ploverville," Milo added.

After finishing their saucers of milk, the group made their way to the library. Like Milo's home, they had to climb a tall winding staircase to get to the main library. The room had thousands of books on shelves along the walls, and all the tables were filled with kumons reading or researching.

Milo led Titus and Constance to the librarian's desk and introduced them to Ms. Kimber, the elderly librarian.

"You must be the famous detectives who are going to help us get the Supreme Book back from the kittens," said Ms. Kimber.

"We are here to determine where the book is," Titus corrected her. "It may or may not have been taken by the kittens."

While Titus was asking Ms. Kimber questions about when the book was last seen, who checked it out, and who put it away, young Todd showed up to help with the investigation.

He said, "Hi, my name is Todd. Milo asked me to come over and help."

"Todd, thanks for coming over. I'm Titus and this is my sister Constance. It seems that you were the last kumon to see the book," said Titus. Todd nodded his head in agreement.

"Ms. Kimber, what is the process for checking out the Supreme Book?" asked Titus.

"Well as usual, I have people fill out a form to check out the Supreme Book and they give me their library card. Next, I unlock the cabinet with the key I keep on my belt, then I take the book off the shelf and place it on the table. When the person is finished, I place it back on the top shelf and lock the cabinet," said Ms. Kimber.

"Todd, when you finished using the book, did you give it back to Ms. Kimber?" asked Titus.

"No. She was busy helping another student, so I placed it on the bottom shelf because I could not reach the top shelf," answered Todd.

Titus looked into the cabinet and noticed towards the back of the bottom shelf was a large square hole. "Where does this hole go?" asked Titus.

"Oh, that is the returned book chute that takes the books to the basement to have them checked back in," said Ms. Kimber. "But we checked the basement and the Supreme Book was not there," she added.

"Todd, you are small enough. How would you feel about taking a ride down the chute to see if the Supreme Book may have gotten stuck?" asked Titus.

Todd thought that would be fun, so he let Titus pick him up and drop him down the chute. As Todd was sliding down, he could be heard yelling weeeeeeee all the way to the bottom. Soon, Todd returned up the stairs to the library carrying the Supreme Book.

"Titus, you were right! The book got stuck on one of the tight turns in the chute," Todd said with a big smile.

"Wow," said Ms. Kimber. "The book was here all along, and we were blaming the kittens for stealing it. Now I really feel bad."

"And the mayor was going to go to Ploverville and accuse the kittens of stealing it," added Milo.

"Yes," said Constance. "Just because you can't think of any other way the book could have gone missing doesn't mean you should assume someone stole it."

Ms. Kimber placed the Supreme Book back on the top shelf and locked the cabinet.

Milo, Titus and Constance made their way to the mayor's treehouse and told the mayor that the book had been found. The mayor was tall for a kumon and looked like a cross between a German shepherd dog and a British shorthair cat. He was wearing a black jacket, white shirt and a red bow tie.

"Thank you so much for finding the book," said Mayor Melville. "We may have started a war had I gone to Ploverville to accuse the kittens of stealing the book." Mayor Melville gave Titus and Constance keys to the city and invited them to join the town for a celebration for finding the Supreme Book.

Before Titus could say anything, the mayor's assistant went to the window and blew a large ram's horn. It was so loud that soon, most of the townspeople had come out of their treehouses and were at the fountain in the town center to wait for the mayor to arrive.

The mayor, Milo, Titus and Constance made their way through the crowd and climbed on the stage, which was in front of the fountain.

"Ladies and gentle kumons," the mayor began. "The famous detective Titus and his assistance Constance have found the missing Supreme Book," started the mayor. A loud cheer went through the crowd. "As it turns out, the book wasn't stolen, but it was misplaced in the library. I think we have all learned our lesson not to decide on one idea as the only choice without checking out other possibilities," he added.

"Today, Titus and Constance are our very important guests, so please make them feel at home," the mayor announced, ending his speech.

As Constance and Titus stepped down off the stage, they were mobbed by hundreds of kumons all trying to shake their hands. Milo grabbed them both and slowly pushed his way through the crowd. After thirty minutes, the group finally made it back to Milo's house.

"As you can tell, you are now heroes in Ronsdale Village. Your service will be added to the Supreme Book and will remain there for all time. Anytime you return you will get the VIP treatment, so please come back soon," said Milo. "Where are you going from here?"

"I think we should head to Ploverville to meet with the kittens and see if we can smooth over any problem that may exist between your two cites," answered Titus.

"The country between here and Ploverville is quite beautiful. How about we take my horse and buggy and all ride up there together. That way I can return with the answer from the kittens on your proposal of peace," said Milo.

Titus and Constance thought it would be a nice change from being on the ship, so before heading north, they took the buggy to the dock to talk with the rest of the crew. Harper and Remy didn't mind sailing the ship to Ploverville; however, Evie and Millie wanted to go in the buggy instead of staying on the ship.

The main road to Ploverville ran right through the center of Ronsdale. As they made their way through the town, a crowd cheered as they passed. Evie and Millie had no idea why the crowd was cheering but waved to everyone anyway as if they were in a parade.

Once they got through town, Evie asked Constance why people were cheering. Constance explained how Titus, using his detective mind, found the missing Supreme Book, which was essential to the kumons.

The road out of town was lined with tall cypress trees on both sides. Past the trees were vast fields of corn on one side and strawberries on the other. As they made it to the top of a hill, they could see the USS Puffin sailing north. Evie waved to the ship, but Harper and Remy were too busy navigating to notice.

"How far is it to Ploverville?" asked Evie.

"About an hour buggy ride," replied Milo.

While they were riding, Milo told the group about the dreaded kittens of Ploverville. It seems that a small group of kittens never accepted the kumons moving in south of them. The dreaded kittens felt that they were pure kittens while the kumons were a mixture of kittens and puppies. Most of the kittens didn't care and were now friends with the kumons, but the small group of the dreaded kittens still caused problems because they wanted kumons to leave so they could take over their land.

As Milo was telling the story, they were riding down the hill into a small canyon. When they turned the corner to enter the canyon, they found themselves surrounded by well-armed kittens.

"Stop where you are," ordered the giant kitten. Milo stopped the horse and whispered to Titus that these were the dreaded kittens.

"State your business," ordered the giant kitten.

"My name is Titus, and we are on our way to Ploverville to speak with your mayor."

"Why are three real-worlders and a mouse from Puffin Village riding with a kumon? Don't you know we don't like kumons?" responded the giant kitten.

"May I ask your name, sir?" responded Constance in her most pleasant voice.

"If you must know, my name is Thor, and I am the leader of this band."

"Well, Mr. Thor, before we continue our journey, can you take us someplace where we can talk?" asked Constance.

"Follow me. Our camp is deep in the forest," responded Thor, not sure what to make of the group. "But the buggy and the kumon will have to stay here along with one of my guards."

"Are you sure this is smart?" whispered Titus to Constance.

"I think it will be safe," whispered Constance back to Titus.

"Go ahead and go," Milo told the group. "I don't mind staying with the buggy."

Thor and his band of kittens blindfolded Titus, Constance, Evie and Millie and led them deep into the forest. Finally, they reached a clearing and the dreaded kittens removed the blindfolds and made the group sit on logs near a fire.

As Titus looked around, he saw a small village with small houses made up of branches covered with large leaves from tropical plants. In the center of the village was a large fire pit where some of the kittens were cooking something that smelled good.

Thor sat on a log across from them while one of the kittens brought over saucers of milk.

"You know, the kumons also drink milk from saucers," said Titus. "I think the kittens and the kumons have more in common then you think," he added.

"Well, the kittens have been here since the beginning of Dreamland, and the kumons have only been here less than a thousand years. They don't deserve to be on our land," said Thor.

"What would you do with that land if the kumons weren't on it?" asked Constance.

"I don't know," Thor responded. "But I do know it would be better than what the kumons are doing with it now."

"Why don't the dreaded kittens like the kumons?" asked Evie.

Ever since Thor could remember, there had always been a group of kittens that didn't like the kumons but for the life of him, Thor couldn't remember why.

Thor gave the best excuse he could come up with. "We don't like them because they are different."

"Well, I am different," responded Millie in a mousy voice. "Does that mean you don't like me and everyone in Puffin Village?"

"That's not a good comparison. You and your town are mice and kumons are a mixture of dogs and cats," responded Thor. "Besides, you didn't take our land."

"If the kittens own the land south of Ploverville, how did the kumons take it away from you?" asked Titus.

"I see what you're doing," accused Thor. "You are trying to use logic on me and confuse me with facts. Well, that isn't going to work. What are facts when you have years of beliefs to stand behind."

Titus and Constance were confused. Their parents always told them that any conflict can be resolved by sticking to facts.

"No, we aren't trying to confuse anyone. We are actually doing just the opposite. We are trying to use facts to clear up what appears to be a simple misunderstanding," Titus said.

"Wait a minute, are you the real-world detectives that the kumons sent for to find their missing book which they thought we stole?" asked Thor. Before Titus could respond, Thor said, "Of course you are. And now you are trying to use logic on me. Well, I can tell you right now, it won't work. I am too smart to fall for facts."

"Okay, fact one," Titus went on as if Thor didn't say any anything, "the kittens were here before the kumons."

"That is true," responded Thor.

"Fact two. The kittens never lived on the land south of Ploverville, right?" asked Titus.

"True, but it doesn't mean the kumons can have it," answered Thor.

"Fact three. The kumons have always been friendly to the kittens of Ploverville."

"Yes, but that's because they know they are on our land," responded Thor.

"Fact four. The kumons aren't any better than the kittens, just different," asked Titus.

"That is also true. If anything, the kittens are better than the kumons since we are pure cats," answered Thor, beginning to like this game. "Kumons are only half cats."

Titus continued talking and said, "Fact five. The kittens have more than enough land and even if the kumons weren't on the land, chances are the kittens wouldn't be using it."

"True," Thor answered. "We do have more than enough land."

"So, if the kittens have no use for the land, and if the kumons have been good neighbors, and if the kittens feel that they are better than the kumons, why not just forget the past and become friends now?" asked Titus.

"Well, we can't just forget the past and start liking the kumons simply because they are good neighbors living on land we wouldn't use if we had it," responded Thor. He paused after hearing what he said, and it was clear that he was beginning to understand how his answer wasn't logical.

While this discussion was going on, Harper and Remy rounded the peninsula heading toward Ploverville when Harper saw the parrot pirate ship with all of the cannons out, waiting for them.

"Pull alongside us and let us board your ship, or we will blast you to the bottom of the ocean!" shouted captain Paulie, through a megaphone. Harper and Remy had no choice but to allow the parrots to board the ship.

"Where are the real-worlders who lied to me?" asked Paulie.

"They are ashore, and they didn't lie to you," responded Harper.

"You asked them where the treasure chest was, and Titus told you it was at the bottom of the ocean. Did you find the chest?" asked Remy.

"Yes, but it was full of rocks! I wanted the treasure, not the chest," responded Paulie.

Knowing that they were going to have to give up the treasure or be sunk, Remy played along. "Well, why did you ask where treasure chest was and not where the treasure was?"

The parrot squawked and said, "Okay, I will tell you what. If you tell me where the TREASURE is, I will let you go."

"It is in the apple barrel," answered Remy. "All you had to do was ask."

Paulie was mad at himself for being so easily tricked by the real-worlders. He sent one of the pirate parrots below deck to check and sure enough, he found the treasure.

Paulie kept his word. After the treasure-filled apple barrel was loaded on the pirate ship, he let Harper and Remy go on their way.

"Titus and Constance won't be happy about this," said Harper.

"Titus and Constance don't need treasure in Dreamland because they can't take it back to the real-world. Besides, he can always dream about another treasure hunt in the future," said Remy.

Meanwhile, back with the dreaded kittens, Thor ran out of excuses for not liking the kumons.

"Well, let's say you are right about the kumons. If we start liking the kumons, then who should we start to not like? The mice of Puffin Village?" Thor asked, looking at Millie.

"Why do you have to dislike anyone?" asked Constance.

"I don't know, but it seems like we have always disliked the kumons, so if not them then who?" asked Thor.

"Maybe it is time to let go of the belief that you have to dislike a group just because they are different. Start a new belief where you want to get along with everyone," said Constance. "It won't happen overnight, but when it does, you will feel better and be happier."

Thor called a meeting of all of the dreaded kittens and discussed Titus and Constance's proposal. After the meeting, Thor came up to Titus and Constance and said the rest of the dreaded kittens agreed to start liking the kumons. They also decided that they should no longer be addressed as the dreaded kittens. From now on they wanted to be called the friendly kittens of Ploverville.

Everyone shook hands and Thor showed them the way back to the buggy. Once there, Thor went over to Milo, shook his hand and told Milo that he and the other kumons were now the friends of the kittens and that the trading between the two towns would begin again.

"When you see the mayor, please tell him what happened here and that we are now friends with the kumons," said Thor as he walked back into the woods.

"That was quite a meeting you had," said Milo. "How did you change their minds?"

"Elementary, my dear Milo. I just used logic to present the facts," said Titus using a line he remembered for Sherlock Holmes. Suddenly, Titus, Constance and Evie woke up and disappeared from Dreamland.

CHAPTER 19

Ploverville

That night at dinner, Jack asked if Titus and Constance found the missing book in their dream last night.

"Not only did we find the book, which was in the library the whole time, but I think we smoothed things out between the dreaded kittens of Ploverville and the kumons of Ronsdale," Titus said.

"Why were the dreaded kittens mad at the kumons?" asked Jack.

"According to Milo, the kittens thought they were better than the kumons because they were all kittens and the kumons were a mixture of kittens and puppies," answered Titus.

"Being different is just that," said Jack. "It doesn't make you better or worse, it makes you not the same. Can you imagine how boring things would be if everyone were the same?"

"Well, as it turned out Thor, the leader of the dreaded kittens, didn't even remember why the kittens were mad at the kumons anyway. He just remembered that the kittens have always been mad at the kumons, so he and his band of dreaded kittens were mad too. After

Titus talked with the kittens, they decided to be friends with the kumons," added Constance.

"What are your plans for tonight's dream?" Jack asked.

"We will probably ride into Ploverville to meet the mayor and explain that the dreaded kittens are no longer mad at the kumons," said Titus.

Constance added, "I love kittens so I would like to look around Ploverville and meet more kittens."

That evening when everyone fell asleep, Titus, Constance and Evie returned to Dreamland. When they reappeared on the buggy, Millie was sitting next to Milo sharing stories about Ronsdale and Puffin Village.

"You're back," said Milo. "Good timing! We are just entering Ploverville. Millie and I have been getting to know each other while you were gone."

As they pulled into town, Milo asked a cute little calico kitten how to get to the mayor's office. The little kitten told Milo that the mayor wasn't in his office. He was overseeing the annual village treasure hunt.

The little kitten said, "My name is Cloe. Would you like to be on my team for the treasure hunt? The prize is a year's worth of the best cat food that Ploverville has to offer."

Occasionally, Milo ate cat food, but the prize didn't really interest the rest of the group.

"Can other people help you on the treasure hunt?" asked Evie.

"Yes. Some large groups are working together. If they win, they will split the food," replied Cloe.

"Well, since we have to wait for the mayor anyway, we will be happy to help you. How does the hunt work?" asked Titus.

"We all meet at the village center at noon and the mayor gives a clue. After that, we need to use the clue to find the next clue and so on until we find the envelope that says winner on it," explained Cloe.

"Okay, hop in!" said Milo. "It is almost noon, so we better hurry."

Just after they dropped the horse and buggy off at the stable and tipped the stable kitten a dollar to take care of the horse for the evening, the group walked to the village center as the mayor was giving the first clue. The village was mobbed with kittens and cats of all colors and sizes.

Mayor Earl Grey stated, "Here is the first clue to start the annual treasure hunt off. Remember you only have four hours to find the treasure. After that the prize will be put away for the next year."

Like most mayors of that time, Mayor Grey was all dressed up in a black pinstriped three-piece suit, with a black top hat, which made him look very smart.

"The first clue is: hurry up and wait," the mayor said.

Everyone looked at each other with no idea what that meant. Constance looked at Titus and she could tell Titus was still thinking like Sherlock Holmes. Without attracting the attention of the other treasure hunters, Titus whispered in Cloe's ear, "Does your train station have a waiting room?"

Cloe's face had a big smile on it. She said, "Yes it does. Follow me."

So, as the rest of the hunters thought they needed to wait at the village center for the next clue, Cloe led the group down a small alley and into the back entrance of the train station waiting room.

"Now what?" asked Cloe.

"If the contest started at noon and part of the clue was hurry up, let's see when the next train is arriving," suggested Titus.

On the board that announced the train schedule, the next train to arrive was the train from Puffin Village. Under the name of the train was the next clue: The sun only shines in the afternoon.

"That doesn't make any sense," said Evie. "The sun shines all day, even when it is cloudy."

While Titus was thinking, Constance went outside to see what was happening. Most of the cats and kittens were still standing around, waiting for the next clue. A few groups were walking around trying to either figure out the clue or trying to accidentally find it. Across the street, Constance saw the schoolhouse which had a playground and a well. Kittens were swinging on the swings and some were playing on the see-saw.

"Well it looks like the kittens have recess in the playground," Constance said to Cloe.

"Well?" asked Titus, hearing the word. "That's it! Constance, you figured it out. The clue is in the well. Where is the closest well?"

Both Cloe and Constance responded at the same time telling Titus that the closest well was across the street. Constance couldn't figure out what the clue was but acted like she knew all along. Cloe asked Titus why he thought the clue was in the well.

"Since a well is a deep hole in the ground, the sun will only shine inside the well when the sun is overhead in the afternoon," Titus explained. "Cloe, to avoid attracting attention, go over to the well and look inside where the sun is shining and see if there is the next clue."

Cloe made her way over to the well slowly but found she was too short to look inside. As she was standing next to the well Ms. Betsy, the teacher, walked over to Cloe, assuming she wanted a drink and pulled up the bucket to get Cloe a cup of water. As Ms. Betsy dipped a cup in the water, Cloe noticed on the side of the bucket was written: Black and white. Cloe took the cup of water, thanked Ms. Betsy and went back to the train waiting room.

"On the side of the bucket was written: Black and white," stated Cloe, glad she could help find the next clue. Then Cloe added, "I think I know where the next clue is."

Before anyone could ask her how she had figured it out so fast, Cloe said, "Our blackboard in our school is black and the chalk is white. I think the next clue is on the blackboard," she added.

Everyone thought that made sense, especially since the well could be seen from the waiting room and it was also in front of the school. Cloe again made her way to the playground and then when Ms. Betsy was scolding one of the boy kittens for pulling the tail of a girl kitten, Cloe went into the classroom and walked up to the blackboard. In small letters, on the bottom right of the board, was written: Rhymes with well.

Cloe slipped out the back of the school, made her way through and ally and back to the waiting room. By this time, the room had a few kittens walking around looking for the next clue. Titus, Constance, Evie and Millie were sitting on a bench acting like they were waiting for a train. When Cloe came in, the group stood up and made their way out of the train station and onto the platform where the baggage was waiting to be put on the next train.

Cloe told them that sure enough there was a clue on the blackboard, and it was: Rhymes with well.

"That clue is easy," said Evie. "Bell rhymes with well." As she was about to point to the church bell, which was high over the church

217

near the school, Titus told Evie to put her arm down, so she didn't give the clue away to everyone.

As the group slowly made their way to the church, cats and kittens were running to the train station. Someone had figured out the clue. A couple of kittens were also walking towards the well.

"Looks like we better hurry. I think some of the kittens are finding the clues," said Mille. "I'm pretty fast at climbing stairs, so I will run-up to the bell tower and see if I can find the next clue," Millie added.

Huffing and puffing, Millie came down the stairs and whispered to the group that the next clue was indeed there. It read: Lucky U.

Just then, a group of kittens had found the clue in the well and were running into the schoolhouse.

Everyone was stumped on the Lucky U clue. Since each of the clues were near to the prior clue, Titus looked around to see what was close to the church. Besides the train station and school, the only other buildings close were the hardware store and the stable that they had left their horse and buggy.

Suddenly, Titus knew what the next clue was. When Titus was young, he went into his barn at home while his grandfather was changing the horseshoes on one of the plow horses. After his grandfather was done, he took one of the old horseshoes and nailed it over the door inside the barn. Titus wanted to use one nail to fasten it to the wall, making it hang down like an "n" Instead, his grandfather used two nails and nailed it upside down like a "u." When Titus asked his grandfather why he nailed it upside down, his grandfather told him that when you hang a horseshoe-like an "n" it means you have run out of luck, but when you nail it like a "u", it means you will have a lot of luck.

Just then a group of kittens ran up the stairs of the church. Without an explanation, Titus told the group that they needed to go to the stable. Cloe thought that they were going to get their horse and buggy to leave, so she looked a bit unhappy.

Once they got into the stable and closed the door, Titus turned around and sure enough over the door was a horseshoe hanging like a "u." Under the horseshoe was the next clue: Covered Wagon.

"How did you figure that the clue was in the stable?" asked Cloe delighted that they were still looking for the treasure.

"Hanging a horseshoe upside down is supposed to be lucky," answered Titus. "Hence a Lucky U."

As Titus was explaining this to Milo, Constance looked around the stable for a covered wagon. "I don't see any covered wagons here," said Constance.

Constance remembered stories of families making their way west in covered wagons, so she too was looking for a covered wagon. Sometimes people called them a Conestoga.

As Titus was looking outside to see if there were any covered wagons insight, Cloe noticed an old wagon in the back of the stable with a large cloth cover laying on top of whatever was in it. As she made her way to the wagon, a group of kittens came into the stable looking for the next clue.

Cloe quietly lifted the cover to peek inside and found the wagon was filled with cat food along with a note that had WINNER written in big letters.

"We won, we won!" shouted Cloe. The group looked to the back of the stable, and they saw Cloe standing on the wagon holding up the note.

Soon, everyone knew that Cloe had won, and the mayor came into the stable and congratulated Cloe.

Mayor Grey had the stable kitten bring the wagon out to the front of the fountain, and then the mayor climbed on top of the wagon with Cloe next to him.

"We have a winner," announced the mayor. "It is our own young Cloe." Everyone clapped and cheered for Cloe since she knew almost everyone in town, and they all liked her very much.

"How did you find all the clues so fast?" asked the mayor.

"I had some help from my new friends," answered Cloe pointing to Titus, Constance, Evie, Millie and Milo. "They actually came here to meet with you. I told them you were busy with the treasure hunt, so I asked them to help me until the hunt was over."

As the crowd followed where Cloe was pointing, they noticed for the first time that the group included a kumon. The crowd starting murmuring amongst themselves and some even gave Milo mean looks.

Before the crowd could get worked up, the mayor asked Titus to have the group follow him to his office.

The mayor lowered Cloe down to a couple of large savannah cats. They carried Cloe on their shoulders around town as everyone cheered and congratulated her on her win. With all the celebration, they had forgotten about Milo and that he was a kumon.

Titus and the group followed the mayor through the crowd over to the mayor's office. The mayor sat behind a large desk which was covered with important looking papers and a couple of oil-filled lanterns.

Even though it was light outside, the mayor's office was dark, so he lit both lanterns.

Once everyone was seated, the mayor's assistant brought saucers of milk for everyone.

"Why did you want to meet with me?" the mayor asked Titus while staring at Milo. Titus told the mayor the story about the missing book and meeting with the dreaded kittens. When Titus was all done, the mayor started laughing and told the group that for the life of him, he couldn't remember why the kittens were mad at the kumons either.

With that, the mayor stood up and shook everyone's hand (or paw), even Milo's. He proclaimed that this year's treasure hunt party will also be a time for the kittens of Ploverville to become friends with the kumons of Ronsdale.

By the time the group left the mayor's office, the treasure hunt party was in full swing. Cloe was still being carried around town, and everyone was trying to shake her paw.

The mayor climbed up on the wagon and asked the crowd to quiet down so he could make an announcement.

The mayor introduced Titus, Constance, Evie and Millie. When he got to Milo, he asked Milo to come to stand next to him. With that, the crowd grew quiet and stared at the kumon standing next to the mayor.

"Who is the oldest cat in Ploverville?" asked the mayor. Old grumpy cat Mr. Murphy raised his cane over his head.

"Can you tell the crowd why we are mad at the kumons?" asked Mayor Grey.

Mr. Murphy, the cat who always had a mean look on his face and didn't really like anything or anyone, thought for a minute. As the crowd waited for an answer, Mr. Murphy broke out with a big smile and said, "Now that you mention it, no I don't remember." Then he started to laugh for possibly the first time.

Soon the whole crowd was laughing, probably more at Mr. Murphy's laughter, but also because no one could remember either.

"So, I proclaim today is Peace with Kumons Day," said the mayor and everyone cheered. The mayor handed Milo down to a couple of other tall cats and like he did with Cloe, and the cats put Milo on their shoulders and carried him around town, giving everyone a chance to shake his paw.

While all of this was happening, Harper and Remy were just docking in Ploverville Harbor. Hearing all the noise in the town center, they made their way up the dock and into town, seeing Titus, Constance, Evie and Millie standing on the stage near an old cat. They assumed it was the mayor based on the way he was dressed.

"I wonder what mischief they got themselves into this time?" Remy asked Harper.

"I don't know, but everyone looks happy," responded Harper.

Millie spotted Harper and Remy and told Evie, who in turn told Titus and Constance.

"If you will excuse us, Mayor, I just spotted some friends and we would like to go say hi," said Titus.

The mayor told them to join him at the master table in front of the fountain with his group when they were done. "Then we will officially start the party," he said.

After everyone greeted each other and Titus told Harper and Remy what happened in town, Harper told Titus, Constance and Evie about being attacked by the parrot pirates. They told them they had to give up the treasure because otherwise the pirates would have sunk their ship. Harper thought Titus would be outraged, but instead he laughed and told Harper and Remy that they did the right thing. After all, they can always go on more treasure hunts in future dreams.

Harper and Remy, relieved that Titus, Constance and Evie weren't mad, smiled. Then, they all went to join the mayor at the master table.

As they walked to the master table, they passed tables covered with platters of food. Most of the food looked like the cat food Constance fed their cat at home. Titus, however, found the dessert table and filled his plate full of slices of pies and cakes, along with a few fresh chocolate chip cookies and brownies.

As they were eating, the tall cats brought Milo and Cloe back to the master table. Both had plates with heaps of food and saucers of milk on them.

"So, what are your plans from here?" Milo asked.

"I guess we will head back to the ship when the party is over and make our way back to Puffin Village," responded Titus.

"Would you like to join us?" asked Millie, clearly hoping Milo would say yes.

"I wish I could, but I need to get back to Ronsdale to tell everyone the great new that there is now peace between our two towns," said Milo. "Besides, Ms. Myra will be home soon and I have to start my job of being her pet again."

Millie, clearly disappointed, gave Milo her address and told him to visit any time he comes to Puffin Village.

"I think Ms. Myra will be heading to Puffin Village in the next few weeks to visit some friends, so I will definitely make time to stop by," Milo said.

When everyone was done eating, they said their goodbyes to the mayor and Cloe and made their way to the stable. Once Milo had the horse and buggy ready to travel, everyone gave him a big hug and watched him make his way out of town and back to Ronsdale.

Titus, Constance, Millie and Evie followed Harper and Remy back to the ship. While Harper and Titus were charting the trip back to Puffin Village, Constance and Remy untied the ship and Evie and Millie climbed up to the crow's nest.

With Remy at the wheel, they made their way out of Ploverville harbor. As much as Titus and Constance enjoyed being on land, they also loved sailing the open ocean.

As they were rounding the peninsula, a large white pelican landed on the deck in front of Remy. When the bird opened his mouth, out popped Kim, Harper and Remy's next-door neighbor.

"Kim, what are you doing in the mouth of a pelican?" asked Remy.

"I needed to find you quickly, and Pete the pelican offered to fly me out to your ship," said Kim as she was catching her breath. "It isn't easy breathing in the mouth of a pelican, especially when you are holding your nose since he has fish breath," Kim whispered to Remy.

Constance took the wheel while Remy led Kim into the captain's quarters where Titus and Harper were looking at the map.

"Kim, what are you doing here?" asked Harper, surprised to see his next-door neighbor on the ship.

Evie had disappeared from the crow's nest, and Titus could feel himself starting to wake.

"We heard that Titus and Constance were on the ship sailing towards Puffin Village," said Kim.

"What's the problem?" asked Harper.

"It seems that—" Kim began.

Without hearing the rest of the sentence, Titus and Constance woke up.

CHAPTER 20

Trouble in Puffin Village

"Not again!" yelled Titus. "Just as something was about to happen, I had to wake up," he said out loud.

Constance was not happy either. At breakfast, they both tried to guess what was so important in Puffin Village that Kim needed Titus and Constance to return. As they were eating breakfast, Mrs. Drapkin came in and reminded them that home-school starts tomorrow. "Both of you need to be up, have breakfast and ready for school by 7:00am," she said.

"That means we won't be able to sleep in until Christmas," Titus complained to Constance. This will be Titus' second year and Constance first year in school. Like many families in the 1900s, parents would teach their children at home, rather than have them walk a long distance to school.

All through the day, Titus and Constance tried to guess what was going to happen when they returned to Puffin Village.

"Maybe they lost something and need you to find it," guessed Constance. "Or maybe they are having problems with pirates or another village," she added.

Soon Titus and Constance were having so much fun playing by the lake near their home, they forgot all about Dreamland.

That evening when Jack got home, Constance read from her dream journal. She told her parents about how they made peace between Ploverville kittens and the Ronsdale kumons. Titus added that Kim from Puffin Village landed on the ship in the mouth of a pelican. Kim had started to tell them something about Puffin Village, but they woke up before they found out what it was.

While Titus, Constance and Evie were back in the real world, Kim explained the problem to Harper, Remy and Millie. As it turns out, three very distant cousins from the year 2020 were looking through the attic of their home and found very old Harper, Remy and Millie stuffed animals stored away in an old chest. Along with the animals was a note that said, "Any child that sleeps with these stuffed animals near their pillow at night will be able to enter Dreamland when they fall asleep."

"Is that possible for future kids to show up in the same dream as kids from the past?" asked Remy.

"Well, it is highly unusual," said Harper. "Just think if the cousins met," Harper continued. "The kids from 2020 have smartphones, television, the internet, jets and have even had people land on the moon. The kids from the 1900s don't know anything about those inventions or events, and it could change the future if they did find out about them."

"What are we going to do?" asked Kim. "Also, how are you, Remy and Millie going to be in two different times at the same time?"

"It is clear that we have to keep the cousins from meeting each other," Harper said.

"What if when the future cousins arrive, they come to Puffin Village in the 1900s. Then, we can tell them that they can't bring anything from the future with them or talk about any inventions or events," suggested Remy. "That way, in their dream, the future cousins will be dreaming they are in the 1900s, and we won't have to be in two places at the same time."

"That might work," said Harper.

Right after Harper, Remy, Millie and Kim decided on a plan, the Drapkin kids returned to Dreamland.

"Okay, we have been waiting all day to find out what the problem is in Puffin Village. Please tell us what is happening," asked Constance.

"It is very unusual, but it seems that when we arrive in Puffin Village, there will be other real-worlders there as well, and you all will be in the same dream," Harper tried to explain.

"I didn't think that was possible," said Constance.

"Normally not, but as it turns out, your cousins from the future found us. Well they found your old Harper, Remy and Millie stuffed animals in their attic with a note. They plan on visiting Puffin Village any minute now," explained Harper. "For this visit, they will be traveling back in time, so it is essential that you only talk about your time and never ever talk about the future," Harper added.

Titus, Constance and Evie were very eager to meet relatives, they just never thought they would be from the future. They all agreed not to ask or discuss the future with them.

When the ship reached Puffin Harbor, they tied the ship to the dock and made their way to Harper and Remy's house. Harper told the kids to wait in the house and served them fresh-squeezed lemonade along with cheese and crackers. Harper told them to remain inside until they returned and left with Remy and Millie to go meet the future kids.

"Wouldn't you love to know what the future is like?" asked Evie while they were waiting.

"Yes, but it may mess things up if we know too much. We should spend time teaching our cousins what it is like living in our time instead of learning about their time," responded Titus.

Harper, Remy and Millie made their way to the center of the village to meet their new real-world friends. As they got close to Millie's house, three real-worlders appeared and saw Harper, Remy and Millie coming in their direction.

"Hello, I am Harper. You must be Joel," said Harper introducing himself.

"And I am Remy. You must be Abigail," said Remy.

Before Millie could introduce herself, Bethany went over to Millie and gave her a big hug and said, "My name is Bethany. You must be Millie." Abigail and Joel were amazed to hear Bethany speak because she was too young to talk back home.

They all went into Millie's home and Mrs. Mina, Millie's mother, gave them milk and cookies. Abigail started to ask questions and Harper told them that they will explain how everything works later, but for now, they should know they are in Dreamland and that everything is safe and that nothing can hurt them. Harper also told them that in this dream, they are in the year 1900 and that it is essential not to talk about anything from their time. In future dreams you can either come back to this time or come to Dreamland in their time.

Remy asked if anyone brought a smartphone with them, and Abigail and Joel told Remy they were too young to have their own phones yet, but Joel did have a tablet with him, which Remy said she would keep until they left.

Abigail was nine and the oldest of the group, followed by Joel at six and Bethany at three. All three of the kids were excited to visit a village in 1900, so they had no problem with staying at this time.

"So, what video games do you have?" Joel asked Harper.

Harper said, "In 1900 we don't have electricity to our village yet. We don't have TVs, video games, phones, tablets or any of the fancy stuff you kids now take for granted."

"That sounds boring. What do you do for fun?" Joel asked.

"We read, talk to each other, play outside, go on hikes, swim, ride bikes and lots of other things," Millie said.

"From now on, before going to sleep and coming to Dreamland, try and think of where you want to go and what you want to do that night so you wear the right clothes. Since you are in 1900 for this dream, we will need to go over to Mr. Nordmo's General Store and get you the right clothes for the time."

"Thanks, Mrs. M for the snacks," Joel said to Millie's mom when he got up to leave.

"Maybe we should help Mrs. Mina clean up, Joel," said Abigail. "We do that at home."

"That's all right kids, run along. I will clean up, but that was nice of you to offer," said Mrs. Mina.

As they made it to Main Street, Joel and Abigail started to feel out of place being dressed from their time. Abigail was wearing bright yellow shorts with a white and yellow striped shirt and flip flops for shoes. Joel had on his batman pajamas since he forgot to dress for the dream, and Bethany was wearing a pink onesie with a large bulge in the back from her diaper.

Most of the Puffin Villagers ignored the real-worlders since they were used to some of them coming dressed oddly, but a few young mice pointed and laughed to each other.

All the kids were relieved when they finally arrived at Mr. Nordmo's General Store. Harper helped Joel pick out an outfit, while Remy worked with Abigail and Millie with Bethany.

Soon Joel was dressed in brown shorts, knee-high socks, a white long sleeve shirt, suspenders and a flat wool cap.

"Boy, I would sure have problems if I went around dressed like this in my time," said Joel. "These shorts are itchy," he added.

Abigail selected a yellow dress with white socks, black shoes and a matching yellow bow for her hair. Bethany picked out a white dress with a matching white hat, socks and shoes.

Once dressed, Harper went and paid Mr. Nordmo and then Mr. Nordmo wrapped the other clothes in butcher paper and tied them up with twine.

"Guess they outlawed plastic bags here too," Joel whispered to Abigail.

"Plastic bags haven't been invented yet, dummy," Abigail whispered back to Joel.

On the way back to Harper and Remy's house, they ran into Mayor Downing.

"Who do we have here?" asked Mayor Downing.

"These young real-worlders are distant cousins to Titus, Constance and Evie," said Harper.

"My name is Abigail, and this is my brother Joel and my sister Bethany," Abigail said as she curtsied.

Abigail had seen that done in an old black and white Shirley Temple movie she had watched with her mom one evening.

"Well nice to meet you all. I hope you come back often," said Mayor Downing.

"Did you see the size of his tail?" Joel whispered to Abigail as the mayor turned to leave. "I bet he can hang from a tree branch with it," Joel added in a giggly voice. Abigail just rolled her eyes and ignored him.

As they approached Harper and Remy's house, Harper reminded them not to mention anything about the future. They all nodded.

When they walked in, they saw Titus, Constance and Evie sitting at the table discussing what they wanted to do that day.

Abigail recognized Titus, Constance and Evie from an old black and white photo her parents had scanned to their home computer. They sure looked different in color and in person.

Joel remembered the photo too. "Hey, I have seen a photo of all of you in the Cloud from our—"

Abigail hit Joel in the ribs with her elbow to get him to be quiet.

"Ow, what did you do that for?" Joel asked.

"Don't talk about the future," she whispered to him while smiling at her cousins.

"That's funny. We see all kinds of clouds that look like animals, but never like cousins," Titus responded.

With that, they all got up and introduced themselves.

"Is this your first time in Dreamland?" Constance asked.

"Yes, how about you?" asked Abigail.

"Well it seems like forever, but we have only been coming here for about a month," responded Constance.

As they were getting to know each other, Mr. Springer knocked on the door. "Harper? Are Titus and Constance here?" he asked.

"Yes, they are. Come on in," said Harper.

"Someone stole my roasting nuts from my cart yesterday when I went into the market to get supplies, and I am sure it was the squirrels from Willets again," Mr. Springer said. "Can you help me catch the thieves?" he asked.

"Why do you think it was the squirrels?" Titus asked.

"Maybe because they are mad that they had to pay for the nuts the youngster squirrels knocked over a few weeks back," Mr. Springer guessed.

"Did anyone see any squirrels around your cart?" Titus asked.

"No, but what does that have to do with anything? I am sure it is the squirrels."

"Here we go again," Titus whispered to Constance. "Jumping to conclusions with no proof, just beliefs."

"What type of nuts were you roasting?" asked Joel.

"Chestnuts, why?" asked Mr. Springer.

"Squirrels don't like garlic, so if you were roasting garlic, it couldn't be the squirrels," Joel explained.

"Garlic is not a nut, so that doesn't help much, does it?" Mr. Springer said.

"I'm just saying if you were roasting garlic, then it wouldn't be the squirrels that took them," Joel said.

"Thank you for your insight," Mr. Springer told Joel. "If I wear garlic around my neck, will that keep the squirrels away?" he asked.

"It works on vampires, not sure about squirrels," Joel said.

Changing the subject, Titus suggested that they go to the cart and have a look around.

They made their way through the village to Mr. Springer's nut roasting cart. Sure enough, all the nuts were gone.

Titus looked in the dirt for tracks. He saw lots of mice tracks but no squirrel tracks. Then he noticed tracks that looked like they belonged to a very large squirrel, only they were a little bit different. He and the rest of the group followed the tracks and found an empty chestnut shell on the ground, then he found another shell and another.

"I know what bandit took your nuts and it wasn't a squirrel," Titus said. "It was a raccoon." He remembered seeing raccoon tracks around his ranch at home and they looked like the tracks he just found.

"You're right," added Joel. "I remember watching an episode about raccoons on Wild King—" Abigail kicked Joel in the shin and Joel realized his mistake.

"The raccoons live near Arklay Mountain and throughout the Racoon Mountain Range east of here," said Harper.

Just then a chestnut shell hit Joel in the head. They all looked up and saw a fat raccoon with his cheeks stuffed with chestnuts.

"Oops," said the raccoon. "Sorry I hit you in the head young person."

"Get down from there," ordered Mr. Springer.

"Why? Just because I dropped a shell on the child's head. I said I was sorry," responded the raccoon.

"No, because you stole all of my nuts, you bandit!" said Mr. Springer.

"Who are you calling a bandit?" the raccoon said as he jumped down from the tree. "Just because I have a mask doesn't make me a bandit. My name is Rocco and I am not a bandit."

"You are eating my chestnuts that you stole from my cart. I caught you red-pawed," said Mr. Springer.

"Well, if you would have looked in your cash box, which you left on the cart, you would see that I paid for all the nuts and put the money in the cash box since you were not there," Rocco said a bit mad that he was being accused of stealing.

Mr. Springer forgot all about his cash box. He ran back and checked and sure enough, there was enough money there for all the nuts that were gone. Mr. Springer came back and apologized to everyone and went home feeling wrong about how he jumped to conclusions.

"Now that this mystery is solved, what would everyone like to do now?" asked Titus.

"I'm up for an adventure," said Joel.

"Me too," said Abigail and Bethany at the same time.

"We have had a lot of adventures on the west coast, so our next adventure will be going east," said Titus.

Rocco, overhearing the conversation, told the group that he too was heading east to Rexroad Village. Rexroad is his home at the foot of Arklay Mountain, and he invited everyone to join him.

Harper pulled out a map of the area and noticed that Pelrock river ran from the base of Arklay Mountain to Puffin Harbor.

"Is this river large enough for a ship to sail to your town?" Harper asked Rocco.

"Indeed it is," replied Rocco. "I took a riverboat to get here, as a matter of fact."

"Okie-dokie," said Joel. "I think we have a plan."

The group made their way back to the ship and set sail to Rexroad Village, Rocco's hometown at the foot of Arklay Mountain. With a large crew on board, it took less time to untie the ship from the dock and raise the sails. Harper, Titus, Rocco and Joel were in the captain's quarters looking over the map while Remy was steering the ship.

Bethany, Evie and Millie were up in the crow's nest shouting down directions to avoid other boats, and Constance and Abigail were posted on the bow (front of the ship), keeping an eye out for obstacles like rocks or tree branches.

Titus was showing Joel all the places they had visited so far. Titus pointed out Puffin Village, Mt. Pleasant, Willets, Sanderling Island, Ronsdale and Ploverville. Titus purposely left out Corny Island to save Joel from having to listen to such corny jokes.

Rocco showed the group where Rexroad Village was and how Arklay Mountain was one of the tallest mountains in the Raccoon Mountain range. The mountain range ran the length of Dreamland from north to south.

Next, Rocco pointed out other towns and villages which were on the west side of the mountain range. Rocco also pointed to a small area between where they were and Rexroad Village, call Hamstern Hamlet. He told the group about the county fair they were having this week and thought it may be a nice place to stop on the way to his village.

"Sounds like fun to me," said Joel.

"We can use a few more supplies since we didn't pick up any in Puffin Village before we left," added Harper.

"There are some rocks directly ahead!" yelled Evie down from the crow's nest. Remy steered the ship to the left (port) to make sure she avoided running into them. As she got close to the left bank, a branch from a tree almost knocked Abigail off her feet.

"Duck!" yelled Constance to Abigail just in time to save her from getting hit.

241

"That was close," said Abigail. Just then Abigail saw a large root sticking out from the riverbank and yelled to Remy to turn right (starboard).

After that, it was smooth sailing all the way to Hamstern Hamlet. On the way, they passed farms with fields of corn and wheat as well as orchards of cherries, apples and peaches. They saw cows grazing on rolling hills of green grass and large herds of deer and elk roaming free in the distance.

"Town ahead on the starboard (right)" yelled down Bethany. Everyone came out of the captain's quarters to select the best place to dock. As they were approaching the Hamlet, they saw a dirty looking hamster waving his hands and telling the ship to dock. On the dock were cages full of hamsters stacked five cages high.

Remy and Titus tied the ship to the dock and then leaped onto the dock. The rest of the crew stayed on board but went to the rail to find out what was happening.

The dirty hamster went over to greet Remy and Titus.

"It is about time you got here," said the hamster.

"I think you are mistaking us for another ship," said Titus. "Who are you and who were you expecting?"

"I am Taz, the largest seller of pet hamsters in Dreamland. I am waiting for the ship that was supposed to pick them up this morning to sell at the pet market."

Titus looked over at the cages and most of the hamsters looked happy to be going to new homes, but few were clearly upset.

"Did all these hamsters volunteer to go?" asked Titus.

"What's that to you?" asked Taz

"How many of you want to stay here?" shouted Titus to the hamsters in the cages.

Four dwarf hamsters raised their paws, the rest seemed content to leave.

"How much do you want for the four hamsters who raised their paws? asked Titus.

"Give me $5.00 and you can have all four," responded Taz with his paw out.

Titus proceeded to pay and Taz released the dwarf hamsters.

Titus introduced himself to the little hamsters, which were half the size of the other hamsters.

One hamster stepped forward for introductions. "Hi, my name is Archie. This is my brother Arlo and my two sisters are Alice and Amber," he said pointing to each hamster as he spoke.

"It must be confusing finding their backpacks since they all have the same initials," Joel whispered to Abigail.

"Why did you not want to go?" asked Titus.

"Well, we all thought it would be fun to be pets, but then after we were in the cage, we found out that we would be split up and possibly never see each other again, so we changed our minds," explained Archie. "We told Taz we changed our minds, but he said it was too late and would not let us go."

"I heard you have a fair going on. Want to go with us and show us the way?" Titus asked.

"That sounds like fun. Follow us, we will show you the way," said Archie.

Harper and Remy said they would go ashore to get supplies, and Millie decided to stay on the ship to keep an eye on it while everyone else was gone. The rest of the group hopped off the ship and followed the dwarf hamsters into the hamlet.

The hamster homes were all underground, so except for some stores and restaurants on Main Street, the surrounding area looked like a meadow. Every few feet there were round wooden doors built into the meadow that opened like an outside basement door so the hamsters could enter and leave.

Walking down Main Street, they passed grocery, hardware and toys stores, with a few cafés and restaurants on either side. One café had outdoor seating and it was full of well-dressed hamsters drinking what looked like dandelion tea and munching on some green things.

As they approached the end of the hamlet, they could see the Hamster Fair. There were all kinds of rides, games to play with and food booths.

"That will be 25 cents each to get in," said the large teddy bear hamster at the ticket window. "Once you pay the admission, all rides are free."

Before Titus could get money out, Archie paid for the whole group. "It is the least we can do for you rescuing us," said Archie.

Abigail always wanted to own a hamster, but her parents wouldn't allow her to have pets until she was ten years old. She and Joel ran ahead of the group to the hamster ball runabout attraction. There were over twenty hamster balls of all different colors. Hamsters, inside the balls, were rolling around in what looked like a kid's large swimming pool full of water.

After a few minutes, the hamster in charge of the ride blew a whistle, and all the hamsters came to the ladder and one at a time got out. New hamsters took their place.

Fortunately, there were enough balls for Titus, Constance, Evie, Abigail, Joel, Bethany, Rocco and the four hamsters to each have their own ball and go on the ride at the same time.

Once everyone was locked into their hamster balls, the ride attendant blew his whistle again, and everyone started running in their balls. At first, it took the newcomers some time to figure out how to stand up and run. Soon everyone was running into each other and falling in their balls. Joel began laughing so hard that he had trouble standing up. Each time he finally caught his breath and tried to stand up, someone would bump into him and he would fall down laughing again.

The dwarf hamsters, along with some of the long-haired, teddy bear and short-haired hamsters, clearly knew what they were doing. They were all racing around the edge of the pool to see who could go the fastest.

Finally, Joel stopped laughing long enough to stand up and he chased his sisters around in the center, bumping into them every chance he got. Titus went after Joel and hit Joel's ball so hard that the hamster ball spun fast around in circles for almost a minute.

Before they knew it, the whistle was blown, and the ride was over. Joel was so dizzy from spinning in the ball that he fell on the ground when he got out. He lay there until the clouds above him quit spinning. When he got up, he grabbed his stomach because it hurt from laughing so much.

"That was fun," said Joel. "Let's do it again."

"I know something that is even more fun," said Archie. "Follow me."

246

Archie led the group over to what looked like a large wooden hamster wheel. But instead of being vertical like most hamster wheels, the wheel was laying down.

"How does this ride work?" asked Evie.

"When the door opens, you go in and stand with your back to the wall. Then, when everyone is in, the wheel starts spinning," instructed Archie.

Joel couldn't see how that could be as much fun as the hamster balls, but he wanted to try it anyway.

Soon, everyone was in the wheel against the wall, and the ride attendant locked the door. At first, the wheel started spinning slowly, then it picked up speed. As the ride began picking up speed, Joel noticed he was being pushed against the wall. Soon, the wheel was spinning so fast he couldn't move. Even his arms were flat against the wall.

The wheel started to rise and before he knew it, the wheel was vertical. It took all his strength to turn his head to the right to see Abigail. She was pinned against the wall and laughing hard. This made Joel laugh.

Joel turned his head to the other side to see Titus, who was also laughing hard. Titus turned to look at Joel and Joel started laughing all over again. Joel slowly moved his head to look across the wheel and saw Rocco and the four hamsters also laughing.

Finally, the ride ended. Everyone fell to the ground when they got off the ride. After the clouds quit spinning, they stood up. Joel asked if there were rides that don't spin or make him laugh so he could recover.

Archie took the group over to the giant hamster slide. The ride was the tallest attraction in the park. They had to climb up a long ladder, and once they were on top the attendant gave each person a rug to sit on to slide down the wooden tube.

Bethany and Evie went first. You could hear them yell as they descended the slide. The rest of the group followed right behind them. The ride started with a long drop where they picked up speed. Soon there were turns and then a large vertical circle where they went upside down. At the end of the ride, there was a smooth wooden ramp where they slowed down.

"That was fun too," said Joel. "And I am not dizzy."

As they were making their way to the next ride, Evie disappeared.

"What happened to Evie?" asked Bethany.

"Looks like she woke up. We better head back to the ship before we all wake up," answered Constance.

As they were walking to the ship, Constance explained to Abigail, Joel and Bethany about what happens when you wake up. She also told them about her dream journal.

"When you wake up, you leave Dreamland and go back to the real world. It's best to keep a dream journal and write down your dream when you first wake up, so you know what happened and where you want to return for your next dream," explained Constance.

"We know about the dream journal," responded Abigail. "That's how we knew you would be going to Puffin Village today."

Constance couldn't figure out how Abigail could have her journal since she knew she left it in the drawer of her nightstand by her bed.

"When we found your old Harper, Remy and Millie toys, along with the note about how to enter Dreamland, in our attic, we also found your journal. Don't forget we live a hundred and twenty years in the future from your time, so we know about all the adventures you, Titus and Evie went on," explained Abigail.

Constance almost forgot that Abigail, Joel and Bethany were from the future, which made sense why Abigail had her dream journal.

"So, who is the president in your time?" asked Joel who was now part of the conversation.

"We promised not to tell you anything about the future, and anyway, you would not believe me if I told you about our president," responded Titus.

"Joel and I have agreed not to read ahead in your journal from this point on, so if we end up joining you in the future, we won't know how the dream turns out. We will only read enough to find out where you are," said Abigail.

"Do you plan on joining us on future adventures?" asked Titus.

"Joel and I talked things over, and we decided we like the year 1900 so much that we plan on coming back to this time when we dream. From time to time, we will join you if that is okay with you."

"Of course, we would love to have you join us on some adventures," said Titus, looking at Constance to make sure she agreed, which she did.

At the dock, everyone thanked Archie and his brother and sisters. They all hugged and promised to return in a future dream.

Harper, Remy and Millie had the ship stocked and ready to go.

As soon as they cast off, Constance and Titus woke up and disappeared.

That morning at breakfast, Constance and Titus talked about how much fun they had with their future cousins and how they hoped to go on more adventures with them.

The End.

Look for Book Two: The Jenkin Kids go to Dreamland

Made in the USA
Lexington, KY
07 December 2019